Lesley spun away from the mirror suddenly as she heard the door open and saw Alessio look at her in shock.

"What are you doing here?" She felt naked as his eyes slowly raked over her from the top of her head, along her body and then all the way back again.

Alessio couldn't stop looking at her. Any other woman would have been overjoyed to be the center of his attention, as she now was, but instead she was staring straight ahead, unblinking, doing her utmost to shut him out of her line of vision.

He had never wanted a woman as much as he wanted this one right now. Mind and body fused. This wasn't just another of his glamorous, sex-kitten women. This thinking, questioning, irreverent creature was in a different league.

All about the author...
Cathy Williams

CATHY WILLIAMS was born in the West Indies and has been writing Harlequin® romances for some fifteen years. She is a great believer in the power of perseverance, as she had never written anything before (apart from school essays a lifetime ago!), and from the starting point of zero has now fulfilled her ambition to pursue this most enjoyable of careers. She would encourage any would-be writer to have faith and go for it! She lives in the beautiful Warwickshire countryside with her husband and three children, Charlotte, Olivia and Emma. When not writing she is hard-pressed to find a moment's free time in between the millions of household chores, not to mention being a one-woman taxi service for her daughters' never-ending social lives. She derives inspiration from the hot, lazy, tropical island of Trinidad (where she was born), from the peaceful countryside of middle England and, of course, from her many friends, who are a rich source of plots and are particularly garrulous when it comes to describing Harlequin Presents® heroes. It would seem, from their complaints, that tall, dark and charismatic men are way too few and far between. Her hope is to continue writing romance fiction, providing those eternal tales of love for which, she feels, we all strive.

Other titles by Cathy Williams available in ebook:

THE ARGENTINIAN'S DEMAND
SECRETS OF A RUTHLESS TYCOON
ENTHRALLED BY MORETTI
HIS TEMPORARY MISTRESS

Cathy Williams

The Uncompromising Italian

Recycling programs for this product may not exist in your area.

ISBN-13: 978-0-373-13284-3

THE UNCOMPROMISING ITALIAN

First North American Publication 2014

This edition published by arrangement with Harlequin Books S.A.

For questions and comments about the quality of this book, please contact us at CustomerService@Harlequin.com.

HARLEQUIN®
www.Harlequin.com

Printed in U.S.A.

The Uncompromising Italian

To my wonderful daughters.

CHAPTER ONE

LESLEY FOX SLOWLY drew to a stop in front of the most imposing house she had ever seen.

The journey out of London had taken barely any time at all. It was Monday, it was the middle of August and she had been heading against the traffic. In all it had taken her under an hour to leave her flat in crowded Ladbroke Grove and arrive at a place that looked as though it should be plastered on the cover of a *House Beautiful* magazine.

The wrought-iron gates announced its splendour, as had the tree-lined avenue and acres of manicured lawns through which she had driven.

The guy was beyond wealthy. Of course, she had known that. The first thing she had done when she had been asked to do this job had been to look him up online.

Alessio Baldini—Italian, but resident in the UK for a long time. The list of his various companies was vast and she had skipped over all of that. What he did for a living was none of her business. She had just wanted to make sure that the man existed and was who Stan said he was.

Commissions via friends of friends were not always to be recommended, least of all in her niche sideline business. A girl couldn't be too careful, as her father liked to say.

She stepped out of her little Mini, which was dwarfed in the vast courtyard, and took a few minutes to look around her.

The brilliance of a perfect summer's day made the sprawling green lawns, the dense copse to one side lush with lavender and the clambering roses against the stone of the mansion facing her seem almost too breathtakingly beautiful to be entirely real.

This country estate was in a league of its own.

There had been a bit of information on the Internet about where the man lived, but no pictures, and she had been ill-prepared for this concrete display of wealth.

A gentle breeze ruffled her short brown hair and for once she felt a little awkward in her routine garb of lightweight combat trousers, espadrilles and one of her less faded tee-shirts advertising the rock band she had gone to see five years ago.

This didn't seem the sort of place where dressing down would be tolerated.

For the first time, she wished she had paid a little more attention to the details of the guy she was going to see.

There had been long articles about him but few pictures and she had skimmed over those, barely noting which one he was amidst the groups of boring men in business suits who'd all seemed to wear the identical smug smiles of people who had made far too much money for their own good.

She grabbed her laptop from the passenger seat and slammed the door shut.

If it weren't for Stan, she wouldn't be here now. She didn't need the money. She could afford the mortgage on her one-bedroom flat, had little interest in buying pointless girly clothes for a figure she didn't possess to attract men in whom she had scant interest—or who, she amended with scrupulous honesty to herself, had scant interest in *her*—and she wasn't into expensive, long-haul holidays.

With that in mind, she had more than enough to be going on with. Her full-time job as a website designer paid well and, as far as she was concerned, she lacked for nothing.

But Stan was her dad's long-time friend from Ireland. They had grown up together. He had taken her under his wing when she had moved down to London after university and she owed him.

With any luck, she would be in and out of the man's place in no time at all.

She breathed in deeply and stared at the mansion in front of her.

It seemed a never-ending edifice of elegant cream stone, a dream of a house, with ivy climbing in all the right places and windows that looked as though they dated back to the turn of the century.

This was just the sort of ostentatious wealth that should have held little appeal, but in fact she was reluctantly charmed by its beauty.

Of course, the man would be a lot less charming than his house. It was always the way. Rich guys always thought they were God's gift to women even when they obviously weren't. She had met one or two in her line of work and it had been a struggle to keep a smile pinned to her face.

There was no doorbell but an impressive knocker. She could hear it reverberating through the bowels of the house as she banged it hard on the front door and then stood back to wait for however long it would take for the man's butler or servant, or whoever he employed to answer doors for him, to arrive on the scene and let her in.

She wondered what he would look like. Rich and Italian, so probably dark-haired with a heavy accent. Possibly short, which would be a bit embarrassing, because she was five-eleven and a half and likely to tower over him—never a good thing. She knew from experience that men hated women who towered over them. He would probably be quite dapper, kitted out in expensive Italian gear and wearing expensive Italian footwear. She had no idea what either might look like but it was safe to say that trainers and old clothes would not feature on the sartorial menu.

She was fully occupied amusing herself with a variety of mental pictures when the door was pulled open without warning.

For a few seconds, Lesley Fox lost the ability to speak. Her lips parted and she stared. Stared in a way she had never stared at any man in her life before.

The guy standing in front of her was, quite simply, beautiful. Taller than her by a few inches, and wearing faded jeans and a navy-blue polo shirt, he was barefoot. Raven-black hair was combed back from a sinfully sexy face. His eyes were as black as his hair and lazily returned her stare, until she felt the blood rush to her face and she returned to Planet Earth with a feeling of sickening embarrassment.

'Who are you?'

His cool, rich, velvety voice galvanised her senses back into working order and she cleared her throat and reminded herself that she wasn't the type of girl who had ever been daunted by a guy, however good-looking he was. She came from a family of six and she was the only girl. She had been brought up going to rugby matches, watching the football on television, climbing trees and exploring the glorious countryside of wild Ireland with brothers who hadn't always appreciated their younger sister tagging along.

She had always been able to handle the opposite sex. She had lived her life being one of the lads, for God's sake!

'I'm here about your… Er…my name's Lesley Fox.' As an afterthought, she stuck out her hand and then dropped it when he failed to respond with a return gesture.

'I wasn't expecting a girl.' Alessio looked at her narrowly. That, he thought, had to be the understatement of the year. He had been expecting a Les Fox—Les, as in a man. Les, as in a man who was a contemporary of Rob Dawson, his IT guy. Rob Dawson was in his forties and resembled a beach ball. He had been expecting a forty-something-year-old man of similar build.

Instead, he was looking at a girl with cropped dark hair, eyes the colour of milk chocolate and a lanky, boyish physique, wearing…

Alessio took in the baggy sludge-green trousers with awkward pockets and the faded tee-shirt.

He couldn't quite recall the last time he had seen a woman dressed with such obvious, scathing disregard for fashion.

Women always tried their very hardest when around him to show their best side. Their hair was always perfect, make-up always flawless, clothes always the height of fashion and shoes always high and sexy.

His eyes drifted down to her feet. She was wearing cloth shoes.

'I'm so sorry to have disappointed you, Mr Baldini. I

take it you *are* Mr Baldini and not his manservant, sent to chase away callers by being rude to them?'

'I didn't think anyone used that term any more…'

'What term?'

'*Manservant*. When I asked Dawson to provide me with the name of someone who could help me with my current little…problem, I assumed he would have recommended someone a bit older. More experienced.'

'I happen to be very good at what I do.'

'As this isn't a job interview, I can't very well ask for references.' He stood aside, inviting her to enter. 'But, considering you look as though you're barely out of school, I'll want to know a little bit about you before I explain the situation.'

Lesley held on to her temper. She didn't need the money. Even though the hourly rate that she had been told about was staggering, she really didn't have to stand here and listen to this perfect stranger quiz her about her experience for a job she hadn't applied for. But then she thought of Stan and all he had done for her and she gritted back the temptation to turn on her heel, climb back into her car and head down to London without a backward glance.

'Come on in,' Alessio threw over his shoulder as she remained hovering on the doorstep and, after a few seconds, Lesley took a step into the house.

She was surrounded by pale marble only broken by the richness of a Persian rug. The walls were adorned with the sort of modern masterpieces that should have looked out of place in a house of this age but somehow didn't. The vast hall was dominated by a staircase that swept upwards before branching out in opposite directions, and doors indicated that there was a multitude of rooms winging on either side, not that she wouldn't have guessed.

More than ever, she felt inappropriately dressed. He might be casual, but he was casual in the sort of elegant, expensive way of the very wealthy.

'Big place for one person,' she said, staring around her, openly impressed.

'How do you know I haven't got a sprawling family lurking somewhere out of sight?'

'Because I looked you up,' Lesley answered truthfully. Her eyes finally returned to him and once again she was struck by his dark, saturnine good looks. And once again she had to drag her eyes away reluctantly, desperate to return her gaze to him, to drink him in. 'I don't usually travel into unknown territory when I do my freelance jobs. Usually the computer comes to me, I don't go to the computer.'

'Always illuminating to get out of one's comfort zone,' Alessio drawled. He watched as she ran her fingers through her short hair, spiking it up. She had very dark eyebrows, as dark as her hair, which emphasised the peculiar shade of brown of her eyes. And she was pale, with satiny skin that should have been freckled but wasn't. 'Follow me. We can sit out in the garden and I'll get Violet to bring us something to drink... Have you had lunch?'

Lesley frowned. Had she? She was careless with her eating habits, something she daily promised herself to rectify. If she ate more, she knew she'd stand a fighting chance of not looking like a gawky runner bean. 'A sandwich before I left,' she returned politely. 'But a cup of tea would be wonderful.'

'It never fails to amuse me that on a hot summer's

day you English will still opt for a cup of tea instead of something cold.'

'I'm not English. I'm Irish.'

Alessio cocked his head to one side and looked at her, consideringly. 'Now that you mention it, I do detect a certain twang…'

'But I'm still partial to a cup of tea.'

He smiled and she was knocked sideways. The man oozed sex appeal. He'd had it when he'd been unsmiling, but now…it was enough to throw her into a state of confusion and she blinked, driving away the unaccustomed sensation.

'This isn't my preferred place of residence,' he took up easily as he led the way out of the magnificent hall and towards sprawling doors that led towards the back of the house. 'I come here to give it an airing every so often but most of my time is spent either in London or abroad on business.'

'And who looks after this place when you're not in it?'

'I have people who do that for me.'

'Bit of a waste, isn't it?'

Alessio spun round and looked at her with a mixture of irritation and amusement. 'From whose point of view?' he asked politely and Lesley shrugged and folded her arms.

'There are such extreme housing problems in this country that it seems crazy for one person to have a place of this size.'

'You mean, when I could subdivide the whole house and turn it into a million rabbit hutches to cater for down and outs?' He laughed drily. 'Did my guy explain to you what the situation was?'

Lesley frowned. She had thought he might have been

offended by her remark, but she was here on business of sorts, and her opinions were of little consequence.

'Your guy got in touch with Stan who's a friend of my dad and he... Well, he just said that you had a sensitive situation that needed sorting. No details.'

'None were given. I was just curious to find out whether idle speculation had entered the equation.' He pushed open some doors and they emerged into a magnificent back garden.

Tall trees bordered pristine, sprawling lawns. To one side was a tennis court and beyond that she could see a swimming pool with a low, modern outbuilding which she assumed was changing rooms. The patio on which they were standing was as broad as the entire little communal garden she shared with the other residents in her block of flats and stretched the length of the house. If a hundred people were to stand side by side, they wouldn't be jostling for space.

Low wooden chairs were arranged around a glass-topped table and as she sat down a middle-aged woman bustled into her line of vision, as though summoned by some kind of whistle audible only to her.

Tea, Alessio instructed; something cold for him, a few things to eat.

Orders given, he sat down on one of the chairs facing her and leaned forward with his elbows resting on his knees.

'So the man my guy went to is a friend of your father's?'

'That's right. Stan grew up with my dad and when I moved down to London after university... Well, he and his wife took me under their wing. Made room for me in their house until I was settled—even paid the three months' deposit on my first rental property because they knew that it would be a struggle for my dad to afford it. So, yeah, I owe Stan a lot and it's why I took this job, Mr Baldini.'

'Alessio, please. And you work as...?'

'I design websites but occasionally I work as a freelance hacker. Companies employ me to see if their firewalls are intact and secure. If something can be hacked, then I can do it.'

'Not a job I immediately associate with a woman,' he murmured and raised his eyebrows as she bristled. 'That's not meant as an insult. It's purely a statement of fact. There are a couple of women in my IT department, but largely they're guys.'

'Why didn't you get one of your own employees to sort out your problem?'

'Because it's a sensitive issue and, the less my private life is discussed within the walls of my offices, the better. So you design websites. You freelance and you claim you can get into anything.'

'That's right. Despite not being a man.'

Alessio heard the defensive edge to her voice and his curiosity was piqued. His life had settled into a predictable routine when it came to members of the opposite sex. His one mistake, made when he was eighteen, had been enough for him to develop a very healthy scepticism when it came to women. The fairer sex, he had concluded, was a misconception of stunning magnitude.

'So if you could explain the situation...' Lesley looked at him levelly, her mind already flying ahead to the thrill of solving whatever problem lay in store for her. She barely noticed his housekeeper placing a pot of tea in front of her and a plate crammed with pastries, produced from heaven only knew where.

'I've been getting anonymous emails.' Alessio

flushed as he grappled with the unaccustomed sensation of admitting to having his hands tied when it came to sorting out his own dilemma. 'They started a few weeks ago.'

'At regular intervals?'

'No.' He raked his fingers through his hair and looked at her earnest face tilted to one side… A small crease indented her forehead and he could almost hear her thinking, her mind working as methodically as one of the computers she dealt with. 'I ignored them to start with but the last couple have been…how shall I describe them?…a little *forceful*.' He reached for the pitcher of homemade lemonade to pour himself a glass. 'If you looked me up, you probably know that I own several IT companies. Despite that, I confess that my knowledge of the ins and outs of computers is scant.'

'Actually, I have no idea what companies you own or don't own. I looked you up because I wanted to make sure that there was nothing dodgy about you. I've done this sort of thing before. I'm not looking for background detail, I'm generally looking for any articles that might point a suspicious finger.'

'Dodgy? You thought I might be *dodgy*?'

He looked so genuinely shocked and insulted that she couldn't help laughing. 'You might have had newspaper cuttings about suspect dealings, mafia connections…you know the sort of thing. I'd have been able to find even the most obscure article within minutes if there had been anything untoward about you. You came up clean.'

Alessio nearly choked on his lemonade. 'Mafia dealings…because I'm Italian? That's the most ridiculous thing I've ever heard.'

Lesley shrugged sheepishly. 'I don't like taking chances.'

'I've never done a crooked thing in my entire life.' He flung his arms wide in a gesture that was peculiarly foreign. 'I even buck the trend of the super-rich and am a fully paid-up member of the honest, no-offshore-scams, tax-paying club! To suggest that I might be linked to the Mafia because I happen to be Italian…'

He sat forward and stared at her and she had to fight off the very feminine and girlish response to wonder what he thought of her, as a woman, as opposed to a talented computer whizz-kid there at his bidding. Suddenly flustered, she gulped back a mouthful of hot tea and grimaced.

Wondering what men thought of her wasn't her style. She pretty much *knew* what they thought of her. She had lived her whole life knowing that she was one of the lads. Even her job helped to advance that conclusion.

No, she was too tall, too angular and too mouthy to hold any appeal when it came to the whole sexual attraction thing. Least of all when the guy in question looked like Alessio Baldini. She cringed just thinking about it.

'No, you've been watching too many gangster movies. Surely you must have heard of me?' He was always in the newspapers. Usually in connection with big business deals—occasionally in the gossip columns with a woman hanging onto his arm.

He wasn't sure why he had inserted that irrelevant question but, now that he had, he found that he was awaiting her answer with keen curiosity.

'Nope.'

'No?'

'I guess you probably think that everyone's heard of you, but in actual fact I don't read the newspapers.'

'You don't read the newspapers...not even the gossip columns?'

'Especially not the gossip columns,' she said scathingly. 'Not all girls are interested in what celebs get up to.' She tried to reconnect with the familiar feeling of satisfaction that she wasn't one of those simpering females who became embroiled in silly gossip about the rich and famous, but for once the feeling eluded her.

For once, she longed to be one of those giggly, coy girls who knew how to bat their eyelashes and attract the cute guys; she wanted to be part of the prom set instead of the clever, boyish one lurking on the sidelines; she wanted to be a member of that invisible club from which she had always been excluded because she just never seemed to have the right code words to get in.

She fought back a surge of dissatisfaction with herself and had to stifle a sense of anger that the man sitting opposite her had been the one to have generated the emotion. She had conquered whatever insecurities she had about her looks a long time ago and was perfectly content with her appearance. She might not be to everyone's taste, and she certainly wouldn't be to *his,* but her time would come and she would find someone. At the age of twenty-seven, she was hardly over the hill and, besides, her career was taking off. The last thing she needed or wanted was to be side-tracked by a guy.

She wondered how they had ended up talking about something that had nothing at all to do with the job for which she had been hired.

Was this part of his 'getting to know her' exercise? Was he quietly vetting her the way she had vetted him, when she had skimmed over all that information about him on the computer, making sure that there was nothing worrying about him?

'You were telling me about the emails you received...' She brought the conversation back to the business in hand.

Alessio sighed heavily and gave her a long, considering look from under his lashes.

'The first few were innocuous enough—a couple of one-liners hinting that they had information I might be interested in. Nothing worrying.'

'You get emails like that all the time?'

'I'm a rich man. I get a lot of emails that have little or nothing to do with work.' He smiled wryly and Lesley felt that odd tingling feeling in her body once again. 'I have several email accounts and my secretary is excellent when it comes to weeding out the dross.'

'But these managed to slip through?'

'These went to my personal email address. Very few people have that.'

'Okay.' She frowned and stared off into the distance. 'So you say that the first few were innocuous enough and then the tenor of the emails changed?'

'A few days ago, the first request for money came. Don't get me wrong, I get a lot of requests for money, but they usually take a more straightforward route. Someone wants a sponsor for something; charities asking for hand-outs; small businesses angling for investment...and then the usual assortment of nut cases who need money for dying relatives or to pay lawyers before they can claim their inheritance, which they would happily share with me.'

'And your secretary deals with all of that?'

'She does. It's usually called pressing the delete button on the computer. Some get through to me but, in general, we have established charities to which we give healthy sums of money, and all requests for business investment are automatically referred to my corporate finance division.'

'But this slipped through the net because it came to your personal address. Any idea how he or she could have accessed that information?' She was beginning to think that this sounded a little out of her area of expertise. Hackers usually went for information or, in some cases tried to attack the accounts, but this was clearly... personal. 'And don't you think that this might be better referred to the police?' she inserted, before he could answer.

Alessio laughed drily. He took a long mouthful of his drink and looked at her over the rim of the glass as he drank.

'If you read the papers,' he drawled, 'you might discover that the police have been having a few off-months when it comes to safeguarding the privacy of the rich and famous. I'm a very private man. The less of my life is splashed across the news, the better.'

'So my job is to find out who is behind these emails.'

'Correct.'

'At which point you'll...?'

'Deal with the matter myself.'

He was still smiling, with that suggestion of amusement on his lips, but she could see the steel behind the lazy, watchful dark eyes. 'I should tell you from the offset that I cannot accept this commission if there's any suggestion that you might turn...err...*violent* when it comes to sorting out whoever is behind this.'

Alessio laughed and relaxed back in his chair, stretching out his long legs to cross them at the ankle and loosely linking his fingers on his stomach. 'You have my word that I won't turn, as you say, violent.'

'I hope you're not making fun of me, Mr Baldini,' Lesley said stiffly. 'I'm being perfectly serious.'

'Alessio. The name's Alessio. And you aren't still under the impression that I'm a member of the Mafia, are you? With a stash of guns under the bed and henchmen to do my bidding?'

Lesley flushed. Where had her easy, sassy manner gone? She was seldom lost for words but she was now, especially when those dark, dark eyes were lingering on her flushed cheeks, making her feel even more uncomfortable than she already felt. A burst of shameful heat exploded somewhere deep inside her, her body's acknowledgment of his sexual magnetism, chemistry that was wrapping itself around her like a web, confusing her thoughts and making her pulses race.

'Do I strike you as a violent man, Lesley?'

'I never said that. I'm just being…cautious.'

'Have you had awkward situations before?' The soft pink of her cheeks when she blushed was curiously appealing, maybe because she was at such pains to project herself as a tough woman with no time for frivolity.

'What do you mean?'

'You intimated that you checked me out to make sure that I wasn't *dodgy*…and I think I'm quoting you here. So are you cautious in situations like these… when the computer doesn't go to you but you're forced to go to the computer…because of bad experiences?'

'I'm a careful person.' Why did that make her sound like such a bore, when she wasn't? Once again weirdly conscious of the image she must present to a guy like him, Lesley inhaled deeply and ploughed on. 'And yes,' she asserted matter-of-factly, 'I *have* had a number of poor experiences in the past. A few months ago, I was asked to do a favour for a friend's friend only to find that what he wanted was for me to hack into his ex-wife's bank account and see where her money was being spent. When I refused, he turned ugly.'

'Turned ugly?'

'He'd had a bit too much to drink. He thought that if he pushed me around a bit I'd do what he wanted.' And just in case her awkward responses had been letting her down, maybe giving him the mistaken impression that she was anything but one hundred per cent professional, she concluded crisply, 'Of course, it's annoying, but nothing I can't handle.'

'You can handle men who turn ugly.' Fascinating. He was in the company of someone from another planet. She might have the creamiest complexion he had ever seen, and a heart-shaped face that insisted on looking ridiculously feminine despite the aggressive get-up, but she was certainly nothing like any woman he had ever met. 'Tell me how you do that,' he said with genuine curiosity.

Absently, he noticed that she had depleted the plate of pastries by half its contents. A hearty appetite; his eyes flicked to her body which, despite being well hidden beneath her anti-fashion-statement clothing, was long and slender.

On some subliminal level, Lesley was aware of the shift in his attention, away from her face and onto her body. Her instinct was to squirm. Instead, she clasped her hands tightly together on her lap and tried to force her uncooperative body into a position of relaxed ease.

'I have a black belt in karate.'

Alessio was stunned into silence. 'You do?'

'I do.' She shrugged and held his confounded gaze. 'And it's not that shocking,' she continued into the lengthening silence. 'There were loads of girls in my class when I did it. 'Course, a few of them fell by the wayside when we began moving up the levels.'

'And you did these classes…when, exactly?'

In passing, Lesley wondered what this had to do with her qualifications for doing the job she had come to do. On the other hand, it never hurt to let someone know that you weren't the sort of woman to be messed with.

'I started when I was ten and the classes continued into my teens with a couple of breaks in between.'

'So, when other girls were experimenting with make-up, you were learning the valuable art of self-defence.'

Lesley felt the sharp jab of discomfort as he yet again unwittingly hit the soft spot inside her, the place where her insecurities lay, neatly parcelled up but always ready to be unwrapped at a moment's notice.

'I think every woman should know how to physically defend herself.'

'That's an extremely laudable ambition,' Alessio murmured. He noticed that his long, cold drink was finished. 'Let's go inside. I'll show you to my office and we can continue our conversation there. It's getting a little oppressive out here.' He stood up, squinted towards his gardens and half-smiled when he saw her automatically reach for the plate of pastries and whatever else she could manage to take in with her.

'No need.' He briefly rested one finger on her outstretched hand and Lesley shot back as though she had been scalded. 'Violet will tidy all this away.'

Lesley bit back an automatic retort that it was illuminating to see how the other half lived. She was no inverted snob, even though she might have no time for outward trappings and the importance other people sometimes placed on them, but he made her feel defensive. Worse, he made her feel gauche and awkward, sixteen all over again, cringing at the prospect of having to wear a frock to go to the school leaving dance, knowing that she just couldn't pull it off.

'I'm thinking that your mother must be a strong woman to instil such priorities in her daughter,' he said neutrally.

'My mother died when I was three—a hit-and-run accident when she was cycling back from doing the shopping.'

Alessio stopped in his tracks and stared down at her until she was forced uncomfortably to return his stare.

'Please don't say something trite like *I'm sorry to hear that.*' She tilted her chin and looked at him unblinkingly. 'It happened a long time ago.'

'No. I wasn't going to say that,' Alessio said in a low, musing voice that made her skin tingle.

'My father was the strong influence in my life,' she pressed on in a high voice. 'My father and my five brothers. They all gave me the confidence to know that I could do whatever I chose to do, that my gender did not have to stand in the way of my ambition. I got my degree in maths—the world was my oyster.'

Heart beating as fast as if she had run a marathon, she stared up at him, their eyes tangling until her defensiveness subsided and gave way to something else, something she could barely comprehend, something that made her say quickly, with a tight smile, 'But I don't see how any of this is relevant. If you lead the way to your computer, it shouldn't take long for me to figure out who your problem pest is.'

CHAPTER TWO

THE OFFICE TO which she was led allowed her a good opportunity to really take in the splendour of her surroundings.

Really big country estates devoured money and consequently were rarely in the finest of conditions. Imposing exteriors were often let down by run-down, sad interiors in want of attention.

This house was as magnificent inside as it was out. The pristine gardens, the splendid ivy-clad walls, were replicated inside by a glorious attention to detail. From the cool elegance of the hall, she bypassed a series of rooms, each magnificently decorated. Of course, she could only peek through slightly open doors, because she had to half-run to keep up with him, but she saw enough to convince her that serious money had been thrown at the place—which was incredible, considering it was not used on a regular basis.

Eventually they ended up in an office with book-lined walls and a massive antique desk housing a computer, a lap-top and a small stack of legal tomes. She looked around at the rich burgundy drapes pooling to the ground, the pin-striped sober wallpaper, the deep sofa and chairs.

It was a decor she would not have associated with

him and, as though reading her mind, he said wryly, 'It makes a change from what I'm used to in London. I'm more of a modern man myself but I find there's something soothing about working in a turn-of-the-century gentleman's den.' He moved smoothly round to the chair at the desk and powered up his computer. 'When I bought this house several years ago, it was practically derelict. I paid over the odds for it because of its history and because I wanted to make sure the owner and her daughter could be rehoused in the manner to which they had clearly once been accustomed. Before, that is, the money ran out. They were immensely grateful and only suggested one thing—that I try and keep a couple of the rooms as close as possible to the original format. This was one.'

'It's beautiful.' Lesley hovered by the door and looked around her. Through the French doors, the lawns outside stretched away to an impossibly distant horizon. The sun turned everything into dazzling technicolour. The greens of the grass and the trees seemed greener than possible and the sky was blindingly turquoise. Inside the office, though, the dark colours threw everything into muted relief. He was right; the space was soothing.

She looked at him frowning in front of the computer, sitting forward slightly, his long, powerful body still managing to emanate force even though he wasn't moving.

'There's no need to remain by the door,' he said without looking at her. 'You'll actually need to venture into the room and sit next to me if you're to work on this problem. Ah. Right. Here we go.' He stood up, vacating the chair for her.

The leather was warm from where he had been sitting, and the heat seemed to infiltrate her entire body as she took his place in front of the computer screen. When he leaned over to tap on the keyboard, she felt her breathing become rapid and shallow and she had to stop herself from gasping out loud.

His forearm was inches away from her breasts and never had the proximity of one person's body proved so rattling. She willed herself to focus on what he was calling up on the screen in front of her and to remember that she was here in a professional capacity.

Why was he getting to her? Perhaps she had been too long without a guy in her life. Friends and family were all very good, but maybe her life of pleasant celibacy had made her unexpectedly vulnerable to a spot of swarthy good looks and a wicked smile.

'So…'

Lesley blinked herself back into the present to find herself staring directly into dark, dark eyes that were far too close to her for comfort.

'So?'

'Email one—a little too familiar, a little too chatty, but nothing that couldn't be easily ignored.'

Lesley looked thoughtfully at the computer screen and read through the email. Her surroundings faded away as she began studying the series of emails posted to him, looking for clues, asking him questions, her fingers moving swiftly and confidently across the key board.

She could understand why he had decided to farm out this little problem to an outside source.

If he valued his privacy, then he would not want his IT division to have access to what appeared to be vaguely menacing threats, suggestions of something that could harm his business or ruin his reputation. It would be fodder for any over-imaginative employee, of which there were always a few in any office environment.

Alessio pushed himself away from the desk and strolled towards one of the comfortable, deep chairs facing her.

She was utterly absorbed in what she was doing. He took time out to study her and he was amused and a little surprised to discover that he enjoyed the view.

It wasn't simply the arrangement of her features that he found curiously captivating.

There was a lively intelligence to her that made a refreshing change from the beautiful but intellectually challenged women he dated. He looked at the way her short chocolate-brown hair spiked up, as though too feisty and too wilful to be controlled. Her eyelashes were long and thick; her mouth, as he now saw, was full and, yes, sexy.

A sexy mouth, especially just at this very moment, when her lips were slightly parted.

She frowned and ran her tongue thoughtfully along her upper lip and, on cue, Alessio's body jerked into startling life. His libido, which had been unusually quiet since he'd ended his relationship with a blonde with a penchant for diamonds two months ago, fired up.

It was so unexpected a reaction that he nearly groaned in shock.

Instead, he shifted on the chair and smiled politely as her eyes briefly skittered across to him before resuming their intent concentration on the computer screen.

'Whoever's sent this knows what they're doing.'

'Come again?' Alessio crossed his legs, trying to maintain the illusion that he was in complete control of himself.

'They've been careful to make themselves as untraceable as possible.' Lesley stretched, then slumped back into the chair and swivelled it round so that she was facing him.

She stuck out her legs and gazed at her espadrilles. 'That first email may have been chatty and friendly but he or she knew that they didn't want to be traced. Why didn't you delete them, at least the earlier ones?'

'I had an instinct that they might be worth hanging onto.' He stood up and strolled towards the French doors. He had intended this meeting to be brief and functional, a blip that needed sorting out in his hectic life. Now, he found that his mind was stubbornly refusing to return to the matter in hand. Instead, it was relentlessly pulled back to the image he had of her sitting in front of his computer concentrating ferociously. He wondered what she would look like out of the unappealing ensemble. He wondered whether she would be any different from all the other naked women who had lain across his bed in readiness for him.

He knew she would—instinct again. Somehow he couldn't envisage her lying provocatively for him to take her, passive and willing to please.

No. That wasn't what girls with black belts in karate and a sideline in computer hacking did.

He played with the suddenly tempting notion of prolonging her task. Who knew what might happen between them if she were to be around longer than originally envisaged?

'What would you suggest my next step should be? Because I'm taking from the expression on your face that it's not going to be as straightforward as you first thought.'

'Usually it's pretty easy to sort something like this

out,' Lesley confessed, linking her hands on her stomach and staring off at nothing in particular. The weird, edgy tension she had felt earlier on had dissipated. Work had that effect on her. It occupied her whole mind and left no room for anything else. 'People are predictable when it comes to leaving tracks behind them, but obviously whoever is behind this hasn't used his own computer. He's gone to an Internet café. In fact, I wouldn't be surprised if he goes to a variety of Internet cafés, because we certainly would be able to trace the café he uses if he sticks there. And it wouldn't be too much of a headache finding out which terminal is his and then it would be a short step to identifying the person… I keep saying *he* but it might very well be a *she*.'

'How so? No, we'll get to that over something to drink—and I insist you forfeit the tea in favour of something a little more exciting. My housekeeper makes a very good Pimm's.'

'I couldn't,' Lesley said awkwardly. 'I'm not much of a drinker and I'm…err…driving anyway.'

'Fresh lemonade, in that case.' Alessio strolled towards her and held out his hand to tug her up from the chair to which she seemed to be glued.

For a few seconds, Lesley froze. When she grasped his hand—because frankly she couldn't think of what else to do without appearing ridiculous and childish—she felt a spurt of red-hot electricity zap through her body until every inch of her was galvanised into shrieking, heightened awareness of the dangerously sexy man standing in front of her.

'That would be nice,' she said a little breathlessly. As soon as she could she retrieved her scorching hand and resisted the urge to rub it against her trousers.

Alessio didn't miss a thing. She was a different person when she was concentrating on a computer. Looking at a screen, analysing what was in front of her, working out how to solve the problem he had presented, she oozed self-confidence. He idly wondered what her websites looked like.

But without a computer to absorb her attention she was prickly and defensive, a weird, intriguing mix of independent and vulnerable.

He smiled, turning her insides to liquid, and stood aside to allow her to pass by him out of the office.

'So we have a he or a she who goes to a certain Internet café, or more likely a variety of Internet cafés, for the sole reason of emailing me to, well, purpose as yet slightly unclear, but if I'm any reader of human motivation I'm smelling a lead-up to asking for money for information he or she may or may not know. There seem to be a lot of imponderables in this case.'

They had arrived at the kitchen without her being aware of having padded through the house at all, and she found a glass of fresh lemonade in her hands while he helped himself to a bottle of mineral water.

He motioned to the kitchen table and they sat facing one another on opposite sides.

'Generally,' Lesley said, sipping the lemonade, 'This should be a straightforward case of sourcing the computer in question, paying a visit to the Internet café—and usually these places have CCTV cameras. You would be able to find the culprit without too much bother.'

'But if he's clever enough to hop from café to café…'

'Then it'll take a bit longer but I'll get there. Of course, if you have no skeletons in the cupboard, Mr Baldini, then you could just walk away from this situation.'

'Is there such a thing as an adult without one or two skeletons in the cupboard?'

'Well, then.'

'Although,' Alessio continued thoughtfully, 'Skeletons imply something…wrong, in need of concealment. I can't think of any dark secrets I have under lock or key but there are certain things I would rather not have revealed.'

'Do you honestly care what the public thinks of you? Or maybe it's to do with your company? Sorry, but I don't really know how the big, bad world of business operates, but I'm just assuming that if something gets out that could affect your share prices then you mightn't be too happy.'

'I have a daughter.'

'You *have a daughter*?'

'Surely you got that from your search of me on the Internet?' Alessio said drily.

'I told you, I just skimmed through the stuff. There's an awful lot written up about you and I honestly just wanted to cut to the chase—any articles that could have suggested that I needed to be careful about getting involved. Like I said, I've fine-tuned my search engine when it comes to picking out relevant stuff or else I'd be swamped underneath useless speculation.' *A daughter?*

'Yes. I forgot—the "bodies under the motorway" scenario.' He raised his eyebrows and once again Lesley felt herself in danger of losing touch with common sense.

'I never imagined anything so dramatic, at least not really,' she returned truthfully, which had the effect of making that sexy smile on his face even broader. Flustered, she continued, 'But you were telling me that you have a daughter.'

'You still can't erase the incredulity from your voice,' he remarked, amused. 'Surely you've bumped into people who have had kids?'

'Yes! Of course! But…'

'But?'

Lesley stared at him. 'Why do I get the feeling that you're making fun of me?' she asked, ruffled and red-faced.

'My apologies.' But there was the echo of a smile still lingering in his voice, even though his expression was serious and contrite. 'But you blush so prettily.'

'That's the most ridiculous thing I've ever heard in my life!' And it was. Ridiculous. 'Pretty' was something she most definitely was *not.* Nor was she going to let this guy, this *sex God* of a man—who could have any woman he wanted, if you happened to like that kind of thing—get under her skin.

'Why is it ridiculous?' Alessio allowed himself to be temporarily side-tracked.

'I know you're probably one of these guys who slips into flattery mode with any woman you happen to find yourself confined with, but I'm afraid that I don't go into meltdown at empty compliments.' *What on earth was she going on about?* Why was she jumping into heated self-defence over nonsense like this?

When it came to business, Alessio rarely lost sight of the goal. Right now, not only had he lost sight of it, but he didn't mind. 'Do you go into meltdown at compliments you think are genuine?'

'I…I…'

'You're stammering,' he needlessly pointed out. 'I don't mean to make you feel uncomfortable.'

'I don't…err…feel uncomfortable.'

'Well, that's good.'

Lesley stared helplessly at him. He wasn't just sinfully sexy. The man was beautiful. He hadn't looked beautiful in those pictures, but then she had barely taken them in—a couple of grainy black-and-white shots of a load of businessmen had barely registered on her consciousness. Now, she wished she had paid attention so that she at least could have been prepared for the sort of effect he might have had on her.

Except, she admitted truthfully to herself, she would still have considered herself above and beyond being affected by any man, however good-looking he might happen to be. When it came to matters of the heart, she had always prided herself on her practicality. She knew her limitations and had accepted them. When and if the time came that she wanted a relationship, then she had always known that the man for her would not be the sort who was into looks but the sort who enjoyed intelligence, personality—a meeting of minds as much as anything else.

'You were telling me about your daughter...'

'My daughter.' Alessio sighed heavily and raked his fingers through his dark hair.

It was a gesture of hesitancy that seemed so at odds with his forceful personality that Lesley sat up and stared at him with narrowed eyes.

'Where is she?' Lesley looked past him, as though half-expecting this unexpected addition to his life suddenly to materialise out of nowhere. 'I thought you mentioned that you had no family. Where is your wife?'

'No *sprawling* family,' Alessio amended. 'And no wife. My wife died two years ago.'

'I'm so sorry.'

'There's no need for tears and sympathy.' He waved aside her interruption, although he was startled at how easily a softer nature shone through. 'When I say *wife,* it might be more accurate to say *ex-wife*. Bianca and I were divorced a long time ago.'

'How old is your daughter?'

'Sixteen. And, to save you the hassle of doing the maths, she was, shall we say, an unexpected arrival when I was eighteen.'

'You were a *father* at eighteen?'

'Bianca and I had been seeing each other in a fairly loose fashion for a matter of three months when she announced that her contraceptive pill had failed and I was going to be a father.' His lips thinned. The past was rarely raked up and when it was, as now, it still brought a sour taste to his mouth.

Unfortunately, he could see no way around a certain amount of confidential information exchanging hands because he had a gut feeling that, whatever his uninvited email correspondent wanted, it involved his daughter.

'And you weren't happy about that.' Lesley groped her way to understanding the darkening of his expression.

'A family was not something high on my agenda at the time,' Alessio imparted grimly. 'In fact, I would go so far as to say that it hadn't even crossed my radar. But, naturally, I did the honourable thing and married her. It was a match approved by both sides of the family until, that is, it became apparent that her family's wealth was an illusion. Her parents were up to their eyes in debt and I was a convenient match because of the financial rewards I brought with me.'

'She married you for your *money*?'

'It occurred to no one to do a background check.' He shrugged elegantly. 'You're looking at me as though I've suddenly landed from another planet.'

His slow smile knocked her sideways and she cleared her throat nervously. 'I'm not familiar with people marrying for no better reason than money,' she answered honestly.

Alessio raised his eyebrows. 'In that case, we really *do* come from different planets. My family is extremely wealthy, as am I. Believe me, I am extremely well versed in the tactics women will employ to gain entry to my bank balance.' He crossed his legs, relaxing. 'But you might say that, once bitten, twice shy.'

She made an exceptionally good listener. Was this why he had expanded on the skeleton brief he could have given her? Had gone into details that were irrelevant in the grand scheme of things? He hadn't been lying when he had told her that his unfortunate experience with his ex had left him jaded about women and the lengths they would go to in order to secure themselves a piece of the pie. He was rich and women liked money. It was therefore a given that he employed a healthy amount of caution in his dealings with the opposite sex.

But the woman sitting in front of him couldn't have been less interested in his earnings.

His little problem intrigued her far more than *he* did. It was a situation that Alessio had never encountered in his life before and there was something sexy and challenging about that.

'You mean you don't intend to marry again? I can understand that. And I guess you have your daughter. She must mean the world to you.'

'Naturally.' Alessio's voice cooled. 'Although I'll be the first to admit that things have not been easy between us. I had relatively little contact with Rachel when she was growing up, thanks to my ex-wife's talent for vindictiveness. She lived in Italy but travelled extensively, and usually when she knew that I had arranged a visit.

She was quite happy to whip our daughter out of school at a moment's notice if only to make sure that my trip to Italy to visit would be a waste of time.'

'How awful.'

'At any rate, when Bianca died Rachel naturally came to me, but at the age of fourteen she was virtually a stranger and a fairly hostile one. Frankly, a nightmare.'

'She would have been grieving for her mother.' Lesley could barely remember her own mother and yet *she* still grieved at the lack of one in her life. How much more traumatic to have lost one at the age of fourteen, a time in life when a maternal, guiding hand could not have been more needed.

'She was behind in her schoolwork thanks to my ex-wife's antics, and refused to speak English in the classroom, so the whole business of teaching her was practically impossible. In the end, boarding school seemed the only option and, thankfully, she appears to have settled in there with somewhat more success. At least, there have been no phone calls threatening expulsion.'

'Boarding school…'

Alessio frowned. 'You say that as though it ranks alongside "prison cell".'

'I can't imagine the horror of being separated from my family. My brothers could be little devils when I was growing up but we were a family. Dad, the boys and me.'

Alessio tilted his head and looked at her, considering, tempted to ask her if that was why she had opted for a male-dominated profession, and why she wore clothes better suited to a boy. But the conversation had already drifted too far from the matter at hand. When he glanced down at his watch, it was to find that more time had passed than he might have expected.

'My gut feeling tells me that these emails are in some way connected to my daughter,' Alessio admitted. 'Reason should dictate that they're to do with work but I can't imagine why anyone wouldn't approach me directly about anything to do with my business concerns.'

'No. And if you're as above board as you say you are...'

'You doubt my word?'

Lesley shrugged. 'I don't think that's really my business; the only reason I mention it is because it might be pertinent to finding out who is behind this. 'Course, I shall continue working at the problem, but if it's established that the threat is to do with your work then you might actually be able to pinpoint the culprit yourself.'

'How many people do you imagine work for me?' Alessio asked curiously, and Lesley shrugged and gave the matter some thought.

'No idea.' The company she worked for was small, although prominent in its field, employing only a handful of people on the creative side and slightly fewer on the admin side. 'A hundred or so?'

'You really skimmed through those articles you called up on your computer, didn't you?'

'Big business doesn't interest me,' she informed him airily. 'I may have a talent for numbers, and can do the maths without any trouble at all, but those numbers only matter when it comes to my work. I can work things out precisely but it's really the artistic side of my job that I love. In fact, I only did maths at university because Shane, one of my brothers, told me that it was a man's subject.'

'Thousands.'

Lesley looked at him blankly for a few seconds. 'What are you talking about?'

'Thousands. In various countries. I own several companies and I employ thousands, not hundreds. But that's by the by. This isn't to do with work. This is to do with my daughter. The only problem is that we don't have a great relationship and if I approach her with my suspicions, if I quiz her about her friends, about whether anyone's been acting strangely, asking too many questions…well, I don't anticipate a good outcome to any such conversation. So what would you have done if you hadn't done maths?'

Time had slipped past and they were no nearer to solving the problem, yet he was drawn to asking her yet more questions about herself.

Lesley—following his lead and envisaging the sort of awkward, maybe even downright incendiary conversation that might ensue in the face of Alessio's concerns, should he confront a hostile teenager with them—was taken aback by his abrupt change of topic.

'You said that you only did maths because your brother told you that you couldn't.'

'He never said that I *couldn't.*' She smiled, remembering their war of words. Shane was two years older than her and she always swore that his main purpose in life was to annoy her. He was now a barrister working in Dublin but he still teased her as though they were still kids in primary school. 'He said that it was a man's field, which immediately made me decide to do it.'

'Because, growing up as the only girl in a family of all males, it would have been taken as a given that, whatever your brothers could do, you could as well.'

'I'm wondering what this has to do with the reason I've come here.' She pulled out her mobile phone, checked the time on it and was surprised to discover how much of the day had flown by. 'I'm sorry I haven't been able to sort things out for you immediately. I'd understand perfectly if you want to take the matter to someone else, someone who can devote concentrated time to working on it. It shouldn't take too long, but longer than an hour or two.'

'Would you have done art?' He overrode her interjection as though he hadn't heard any of it and she flung him an exasperated look.

'I did, actually—courses in the town once a week. It was a good decision. It may have clinched me my job.'

'I have no interest in farming out this problem to someone else.'

'I can't give it my full-time attention.'

'Why not?'

'Because,' she said patiently, 'I have a nine-to-five job. And I live in London. And by the time I get back to my place—usually after seven, what with working overtime and then the travel—I'm exhausted. The last thing I need is to start trying to sort your problem out remotely.'

'Who said anything about doing it remotely? Take time off and come here.'

'I beg your pardon?'

'A week. You must be able to take some holiday time? Take it off and come here instead. Trying to sort this out remotely isn't the answer. You won't have sufficient time to do it consistently and also, while this may be to do with unearthing something about my own past, it may also have to do with something in my daughter's life. Something this person thinks poses a risk, should it be exposed. Have you considered that?'

'It had crossed my mind,' Lesley admitted.

'In which case, there could be a double-pronged attack on this problem if you moved in here.'

'What do you mean?'

'My daughter occupies several rooms in the house, by which I mean she has spread herself thin. She has a million books, items of clothing, at least one desktop computer, tablets... If this has to do with anything Rachel has got up to, then you could be on hand to go through her stuff.'

'You want me to *invade her privacy* by searching through her private things?'

'It's all for the greater good.' Their eyes locked and she was suddenly seduced by the temptation to take him up on his offer, to step right out of her comfort zone.

'What's the point of having misplaced scruples? Frankly, I don't see the problem.'

In that single sentence, she glimpsed the man whose natural assumption was that the world would fall in line with what he wanted. And then he smiled, as if he had read her mind, and guessed exactly what was going through it. 'Wouldn't your company allow you a week off? Holiday?'

'That's not the point.'

'Then what is? Possessive boyfriend, perhaps? Won't let you out of his sight for longer than five minutes?'

Lesley looked at him scornfully. 'I would never get involved with anyone who wouldn't let me out of his sight for longer than five minutes! I'm not one of those pathetic, clingy females who craves protection from a big, strong man.' She had a fleeting image of the man sitting opposite her, big, strong, powerful, protecting his woman, making her feel small, fragile and delicate. She had never thought of herself as delicate—too tall, too boyish, too independent. It was ridiculous to have that squirmy sensation in the pit of her stomach now and she thanked the Lord that he really couldn't read her mind.

'So, no boyfriend,' Alessio murmured, cocking his head to one side. 'Then explain to me why you're finding reasons not to do this. I don't want to source anyone else to work on this for me. You might not have been what I expected, but you're good and I trust you, and if my daughter's possessions are to be searched it's essential they be searched by a woman.'

'It wouldn't be ethical to go through someone else's stuff.'

'What if by doing that you spared her a far worse situation? Rachel, I feel, would not be equipped to deal with unpleasant revelations that could damage the foundations of her young life. Furthermore, I won't be looking over your shoulder. You'll be able to work to your own timetable. In fact, I shall be in London most of the time, only returning here some evenings.'

Lesley opened her mouth to formulate a half-hearted protest, because this was all so sudden and so out of the ordinary, but with a slash of his hand he cut her off before any words could leave her mouth.

'She also returns in a few days' time. This is a job that has a very definite deadline; piecemeal when you get a chance isn't going to cut it. You have reservations—I see that—but I need this to be sorted out and I think you're the one to do it. So, please.'

Lesley heard the dark uncertainty in his voice and gritted her teeth with frustration. In a lot of ways, what he said made sense. Even if this job were to take a day or two, she would not be able to give it anything like her full attention if she worked on it remotely for half an hour every evening. And, if she needed to see whether his daughter had logged on to other computer devices, then she would need to be at his house where the equipment was to hand. It wasn't something she relished doing—everyone deserved their privacy—but sometimes privacy had to be invaded as a means of protection.

But moving in, sharing the same space as him? He did something disturbing to her pulse rate, so how was she supposed to live under the same roof?

But the thought drew her with the force of the forbidden.

Watching, Alessio smelled his advantage and lowered his eyes. 'If you won't do this for me…and I realise it would be inconvenient for you…then do it for my daughter, Lesley. She's sixteen and vulnerable.'

CHAPTER THREE

'THIS IS IT...'

Alessio flung back the door to the suite of rooms and stood to one side, allowing Lesley to brush past him.

It was a mere matter of hours since he had pressed home his advantage and persuaded her to take up his offer to move into the house.

She had her misgivings, he could see that, but he wanted her there at hand and he was a man who was accustomed to getting what he wanted, whatever the cost.

As far as he was concerned, his proposition made sense. If she needed to try and hunt down clues from his daughter's possessions, then the only way she could do that would be here, in his house. There was no other way.

He hadn't anticipated this eventuality. He had thought that it would be a simple matter of following a trail of clues on his computer which would lead him straight to whoever was responsible for the emails.

Given that it was not going to be as straightforward as he first thought, it was a stroke of luck that the person working on the case was a woman. She would understand the workings of the female mind and would know where to locate whatever information she might find useful.

Added to that...

He looked at Lesley with lazy, brooding eyes as she stepped into the room.

There was something about the woman. She didn't pull her punches and, whilst a part of him was grimly disapproving of her forthright manner, another part of him was intrigued.

When was the last time he had been in the company of a woman who didn't say what she wanted him to hear?

When had he *ever* been in the company of any woman who didn't say what she wanted him to hear?

He was the product of a life of privilege. He had grown up accustomed to servants and chauffeurs and then, barely into adulthood, had found himself an expectant father. In a heartbeat, his world had changed. He'd no longer had the freedom to make youthful mistakes and to learn from them over time. Responsibility had landed on his doorstep without an invitation and then, on top of that, had come the grim realisation that he had been used for his money.

Not even out of his teens, he had discovered the bitter truth that his fortune would always be targeted. He would never be able to relax in the company of any woman without suspecting that she had her eye to the main chance. He would always have to be on his guard, always watchful, always making sure that no one got too close.

He was a generous lover, and had no problem splashing out on whatever woman happened to be sharing his bed, but he knew where to draw the line and was ruthless when it came to making sure that no woman got too close, certainly not close enough ever to harbour notions of longevity.

It was unusual to find himself in a situation such as

this. It was unusual to be in close personal confines with a woman where sex wasn't on the menu.

It was even more unusual to find himself in this situation with a woman who made no effort to try and please him in any way.

'I was expecting a bedroom.' Lesley turned to look at him. 'Posters on the walls, cuddly toys, that sort of thing.'

'Rachel occupies one wing of the house. There are actually three bedrooms, along with a sitting room, a study, two bathrooms and an exercise room.' He strolled towards her and looked around him, hands shoved in the pockets of his cream trousers. 'This is the first time I've stepped foot into this section of the house since my daughter returned from boarding school for the holidays. When I saw the state it was in, I immediately got in touch with Violet, who informed me that she, along with her assistants, were barred from entry.'

Disapproval was stamped all over his face and Lesley could understand why. The place looked as though a bomb had been detonated in it. The tiled, marble floor of the small hallway was barely visible under discarded clothes and books and, through the open doors, she could see the other rooms appeared to be in a similar state of chaos.

Magazines were strewn everywhere. Shoes, kicked off, had landed randomly and then had been left there. School books lay open on various surfaces.

Going through all of this would be a full-time job.

'Teenagers can be very private creatures,' Lesley said dubiously. 'They hate having their space invaded.' She picked her way into bedroom number one and then continued to explore the various rooms, all the time conscious of Alessio lounging indolently against the wall and watching her progress.

She had the uneasy feeling of having been manipulated. How had she managed to end up here? Now she felt *involved.* She was no longer doing a quick job to help her father's pal out. She was ensconced in the middle of a family saga and wasn't quite sure where to begin.

'I will get Violet to make sure that these rooms are tidied first thing in the morning,' Alessio said as she finally walked towards him. 'At least then you will have something of a clean slate to start on.'

'Probably not such a good idea.' Lesley looked up at him. He was one of the few men with whom she could do that and, as she had quickly discovered, her breathing quickened as their eyes met. 'Adolescents are fond of writing stuff down on bits of paper. If there is anything to be found, that's probably where I'll find it, and that's just the sort of thing a cleaner would stick in the bin.' She hesitated. 'Don't you communicate with your daughter *at all*? I mean, how could she get away with keeping her room—her *rooms*—as messy as this?'

Alessio took one final glance around him and then headed for the door. 'Rachel has spent most of the summer here while I have been in London, only popping back now and again. She's clearly intimidated the cleaners into not going anywhere near her rooms and they've obeyed.'

'You've just *popped back here now and again* to see how she's doing?'

Alessio stopped in his tracks and looked at her coolly. 'You're here to try and sort out a situation involving computers and emails. You're not here to pass judgement on my parenting skills.'

Lesley sighed with obvious exasperation. She had been hustled here with unholy speed. He had even come with her to her office, on the pretext of having a look at what her company did, and had so impressed her boss that Jake had had no trouble in giving her the week off.

And now, having found herself in a situation that somehow didn't seem to be of her own choosing, she wasn't about to be lectured to in that patronising tone of voice.

'I'm not passing opinions on your parenting skills,' she said with restraint. 'I'm trying to make sense of a picture. If I can see the whole picture, then I might have an idea of how and where to proceed.' She had not yet had time since arriving to get down to the business of working her way through the emails and trying to trace the culprit responsible for them.

That was a job for the following day. Right now, she would barely have time to have dinner, run a bath and then hit the sack. It had been a long day.

'I mean,' she said into an unresponsive silence, 'If and when I do find out who is responsible for those emails, we still won't know why he's sending them. He could clam up, refuse to say anything, and then you may still be left with a problem on your hands in connection with your daughter.'

They had reached the kitchen, which was a vast space dominated by a massive oak table big enough to seat ten. Everything in the house was larger than life, including all the furnishings.

'They may have nothing to do with Rachel. That's just another possibility.' He took a bottle of wine from the fridge and two wine glasses from one of the cupboards. There was a rich smell of food and Lesley looked around for Violet, who seemed to be an invisible but constant presence in the house.

'Where's Violet?' she asked, hovering.

'Gone for the evening. I try and not keep the hired help chained to the walls at night.' He proffered the glass of wine. 'And you can come inside, Lesley. You're not entering a lion's den.'

It felt like it, however. In ways she couldn't put her finger on, Alessio Baldini felt exciting and dangerous at the same time. Especially so at night, here, in his house with no one around.

'She's kindly prepared a casserole for us. Beef. It's in the oven. We can have it with bread, if that suits you.'

'Of course,' Lesley said faintly. 'Is that how it works when you're here? Meals are prepared for you so that all you have to do is switch the oven on?'

'One of the housekeepers tends to stick around when Rachel's here.' Alessio flushed and turned away.

In that fleeting window, she glimpsed the situation with far more clarity than if she had had it spelled out for her.

He was so awkward with his own daughter that he preferred to have a third party to dilute the atmosphere. Rachel probably felt the same way. Two people, father and daughter, were circling one another like strangers in a ring.

He had been pushed to the background during her formative years, had found his efforts at bonding repelled and dismantled by a vengeful wife, and now found himself with a teenager he didn't know. Nor was he, by nature, a people person—the sort of man who could joke his way back into a relationship.

Into that vacuum, any number of gremlins could have entered.

'So you're *never* on your own with your daughter? Okay. In that case you really wouldn't have a clue what was happening in her life, especially as she spends most of the year away from home. But you were saying that this may not have anything directly to do with Rachel. What did you mean by that?'

She watched him bring the food to the table and refill their glasses with more wine.

Alessio gave her a long, considered look from under his lashes.

'What I am about to tell you stays within the walls of this house, is that clear?'

Lesley paused with her glass halfway to her mouth and looked at him over the rim with astonishment.

'And you laugh at me for thinking that you might have links to the Mafia?'

Alessio stared at her and then shook his head and slowly grinned. 'Okay, maybe that sounded a little melodramatic.'

Lesley was knocked sideways by that smile. It was so full of charm, so lacking in the controlled cool she had seen in him before. It felt as though, the more time she spent in his company, the more intriguing and complex he became. He was not simply a mega-rich guy employing her to do a job for him, but a man with so many facets to his personality that it made her head spin.

Worse than that, she could feel herself being sucked in, and that scared her.

'I don't do melodrama,' Alessio was saying with the remnants of his smile. 'Do you?'

'Never.' Lesley licked her lips nervously. 'What are you going to tell me that has to stay here?'

His dark eyes lingered on her flushed face. 'It's unlikely that our guy would have got hold of this information but, just in case, it's information I would want to protect my daughter from knowing. I certainly would not want it in the public arena.' He swigged the remainder of his wine and did the honours by dishing food onto the plates which had already been put on the table, along with glasses and cutlery.

Mesmerised by the economic elegance of his movements, and lulled by the wine and the creeping darkness outside, Lesley cupped her chin in her hand and stared at him.

He wasn't looking at her. He was concentrating on not spilling any food. He had the expression of someone unaccustomed to doing anything of a culinary nature for themselves—focused yet awkward at the same time.

'You don't look comfortable with a serving spoon,' she remarked idly and Alessio glanced across to where she was sitting, staring at him. She wore a thin gold chain with a tiny pendant around her neck and she was playing with the pendant, rolling it between her fingers as she looked at him.

Suddenly and for no reason, his breathing thickened and heat surged through his body with unexpected force. His libido, that had not seen the light of day for the past couple of months, reared up with such urgency that he felt his sharp intake of breath.

She was not trying to be seductive but somehow he could feel her seducing him.

'I bet you don't do much cooking for yourself.'

'Come again?' Alessio did his best to get his thoughts back in order. An erection was jamming against the zipper of his trousers, rock-hard and painful, and it was a relief to sit down.

'I said, you don't look as though handling pots and pans comes as second nature to you.' She tucked into the casserole, which was mouth-wateringly fragrant. They should be discussing work but the wine had made her feel relaxed and mellow and had allowed her curiosity about him to come out of hiding and to take centre stage.

Sober, she would have chased that curiosity away, because she could feel its danger. But pleasantly tipsy, she wanted to know more about him.

'I don't do much cooking, no.'

'I guess you can always get someone else to do it for you. Top chefs or housekeepers, or maybe just your girlfriends.' She wondered what his girlfriends looked like. He might have had a rocky marriage that had ended in divorce, but he would have lots of girlfriends.

'I don't let women near my kitchen.' Alessio was amused at her disingenuous curiosity. He swirled his wine around in the glass and swallowed a mouthful.

With a bit of alcohol in her system, she looked more relaxed, softer, less defensive.

His erection was still throbbing and his eyes dropped to her mouth, then lower to where the loose neckline of her tee-shirt allowed a glimpse of her shoulder blades and the soft hint of a cleavage. She wasn't big breasted and the little she had was never on show.

'Why? Don't you ever go out with women who like to cook?'

'I've never asked whether they like to cook or not,' he said wryly, finishing his wine, pouring himself another glass and keeping his eyes safely away from her loose-limbed body. 'I've found that, the minute a woman starts eulogising about the joys of home-cooked food, it usually marks the end of the relationship.'

'What do you mean?' Lesley looked at him, surprised.

'It means that the last thing I need is someone trying to prove that they're a domestic goddess in my kitchen. I prefer that the women I date don't get too settled.'

'In case they get ideas of permanence?'

'Which brings me neatly back to what I wanted to say.' That disturbing moment of intense sexual attraction began to ebb away and he wondered how it had arisen in the first place.

She was nothing like the women he dated. Could it be that her intelligence, the strange role she occupied as receiver of information no other woman had ever had, the sheer difference of her body, had all those things conspired against him?

There was a certain intimacy to their conversation. Had that entered the mix and worked some kind of passing, peculiar magic?

More to the point, a little voice inside him asked, what did he intend to do about it?

'I have a certain amount of correspondence locked away that could be very damaging.'

'Correspondence?'

'Of the non-silicon-chip variety,' Alessio elaborated drily. 'Correspondence of the old-fashioned sort—namely, letters.'

'To do with business?' She felt a sudden stab of intense disappointment that she had actually believed him when he had told her that he was an honest guy in all his business dealings.

'No, not to do with business, so you can stop thinking that you've opened a can of worms and you need to clear off as fast as you can. I told you I'm perfectly straight when it comes to my financial dealings and I wasn't lying.'

Lesley released a long sigh of relief. Of course, it was because she would have been in a very awkward situation had he confessed to anything shady, especially considering she was alone with him in his house.

It definitely wasn't because she would have been disappointed in him as a man had he been party to anything crooked.

'Then what? And what is the relevance to the case?'

'This could hurt my daughter. It would certainly be annoying for me should it hit the press. If I fill you in, then you might be able to join some dots and discover if this is the subject of his emails.'

'You have far too much confidence in my abilities, Mr Baldini.' She smiled. 'I may be good at what I do but I'm not a miracle worker.'

'I think we've reached the point where you can call me Alessio. It occurred to me that there may have been stray references in the course of the emails that might point in a certain direction.'

'And you feel that I need to know the direction they may point in so that I can pick them up if they're there?'

'Something like that.'

'Wouldn't you have seen them for yourself?'

'I only began paying attention to those emails the day you were hired. Before that, I had kept them, but hadn't examined them in any depth and I haven't had the opportunity to do so since. It's a slim chance but we can cover all bases.'

'And what if I do find a link?'

'Then I shall know what options to take when it comes to dealing with the perpetrator.'

Lesley sighed and fluffed her short hair up with her fingers. 'Do you know, I have never been in this sort of situation before.'

'But you've had a couple of tricky occasions.'

'Not as complicated as this. The tricky ones have usually involved friends of friends imagining that I can unearth marital affairs by bugging computers, and then

I have to let them down. If I can even be bothered to see what they want in the first place.'

'And this?'

'This feels as though it's got layers.' And she wasn't sure that she wanted to peel them back to see what was lying underneath. It bothered her that he had such an effect on her that he had been able to entice her into taking time off work to help him in the first place.

And it bothered her even more that she couldn't seem to stop wanting to stare at him. Of course he was good-looking, but she was sensible when it came to guys, and this one was definitely off-limits. The gulf between them was so great that they could be living on different planets.

And yet her eyes still sought him out, and that was worrying.

'I had more than one reason for divorcing my wife,' he said heavily, after a while. He hesitated, at a loss as to where to go from there, because sharing confidences was not something he ever did. From the age of eighteen, he had learnt how to keep his opinions to himself—first through a sense of shame that he had been hoodwinked by a girl he had been seeing for a handful of months, a girl who had conned him into thinking she had been on the pill. Later, when his marriage had predictably collapsed, he had developed a forbidding ability to keep his emotions and his thoughts under tight rein. It was what he had always seen as protection against ever making another mistake when it came to the opposite sex.

But now…

Her intelligent eyes were fixed on his face. He reminded himself that this was a woman against whom he needed no protection because she had no ulterior agenda.

'Not only did Bianca lie her way into a marriage but she also managed to lie her way into making me believe that she was in love with me.'

'You were a kid,' Lesley pointed out, when he failed to elaborate on that remark. 'It happens.'

'And you know because…?'

'I don't,' she said abruptly. 'I wasn't one of those girls anyone lied to about being in love with. Carry on.'

Alessio tilted his head and looked at her enquiringly, tempted to take her up on that enigmatic statement, even though he knew he wouldn't get anywhere with it.

'We married and, very shortly after Rachel was born, my wife began fooling around. Discreetly at first, but that didn't last very long. We moved in certain circles and it became a bore to try and work out who she wanted to sleep with and when she would make a move.'

'How awful for you.'

Alessio opened his mouth to brush that show of sympathy to one side but instead stared at her for a few moments in silence. 'It wasn't great,' he admitted heavily.

'It can't have been. Not at any age, but particularly not when you were practically a child yourself and not equipped to deal with that kind of disillusionment.'

'No.' His voice was rough but he gave a little shrug, dismissing that episode in his life.

'I can understand why you would want to protect your daughter from knowing that her mother was… promiscuous.'

'There's rather more.' His voice was steady and matter-of-fact. 'When our marriage was at its lowest ebb, Bianca implied, during one of our rows, that I wasn't Rachel's father at all. Afterwards she retracted her words and said that she hadn't been thinking straight. God knows, she probably realised that Rachel was her lifeline to money, and the last thing she should do was to jeopardise that lifeline, but the words were out and as far as I was concerned couldn't be taken back.'

'No, I can understand that.' Whoever said that money could buy happiness? she thought, feeling her heart constrict for the young boy he must have been then—deceived, betrayed, cheated on; forced to become a man when he was still in his teens.

'One day when she was out shopping, I returned early from work and decided, on impulse, to go through her drawers. By this time, we were sleeping in separate rooms. I found a stash of letters, all from the same guy, someone she had known when she was sixteen. Met him on holiday somewhere in Majorca. Young love. Touching, don't you think? They kept in contact and she was seeing him when she was married to me. I gathered from reading between the lines that he was the son of a poor fisherman, someone her parents would certainly not have welcomed with open arms.'

'No.'

'The lifestyles of the rich and famous,' he mocked wryly. 'I bet you're glad you weren't one of the privileged crowd.'

'I never gave it much thought, but now that you mention it…' She smiled and he grudgingly returned the smile.

'I have no idea whether the affair ended when her behaviour became more out of control but it certainly made me wonder whether she was right about our daughter not being biologically mine. Not that it would have made a scrap of difference but…'

'You'd have to find out that sort of thing.'

'Tests proved conclusively that Rachel is my child but you can see why this information could be highly destructive if it came to light, especially considering the poor relationship I have with my daughter. It could be catastrophic. She would always doubt my love for her if she thought that I had taken a paternity test to prove she was mine in the first place. It would certainly destroy the happy memories she has of her mother and, much as Bianca appalled me, I wouldn't want to deprive Rachel of her memories.'

'But if this information was always private and historic, and only contained in letter form, then I don't see how anyone else could have got hold of it.' But there were always links to links to links; it just took one person to start delving and who knew what could come out in the wash? 'I'll see if I can spot any names or hints that this might be the basis of the threats.'

And at the same time, she would have her work cut out going through his daughter's things, a job which still didn't sit well with her, even though a part of her know that it was probably essential.

'I should be heading up to bed now,' she said, rising to her feet.

'It's not yet nine-thirty.'

'I'm an early-to-bed kind of person,' she said awkwardly, not knowing whether to leave the kitchen or remain where she was, then realising that she was behaving like an employee waiting for her boss to dismiss her. But her feet remained nailed to the spot.

'I have never talked so much about myself,' Alessio murmured, which got her attention, and she looked at him quizzically. 'It's not in my nature. I'm a very private man, hence what I've told you goes no further than this room.'

'Of course it won't,' Lesley assured him vigorously. 'Who would I tell?'

'If someone could consider blackmailing me over this information, then it might occur to you that you could do the same. You would certainly have unrivalled proof of whatever you wanted to glean about my private life in the palm of your hand.'

It was a perfectly logical argument and he was, if nothing else, an extremely logical man. But Alessio still felt an uncustomary twinge of discomfort at having spelled it out so clearly.

He noticed the patches of angry colour that flooded her cheeks and bit back the temptation to apologise for being more blunt than strictly necessary.

She worked with computers; she would know the value of logic and reason.

'You're telling me that you don't trust me.'

'I'm telling you that you keep all of this to yourself. No girly gossip in the toilets at work, or over a glass of wine with your friends, and certainly no pillow talk with whoever you end up sharing your bed with.'

'Thank you for spelling it out so clearly,' Lesley said coldly. 'But I know how to keep a confidence and I fully understand that it's important that none of this gets out. If you have a piece of paper, you can draft something up right here and I'll sign it!'

'Draft something up?' Under normal circumstances, he certainly would have had that in place before hiring her for the job, but for some reason it simply hadn't occurred to him.

Perhaps it had been the surprise of opening the front door to a girl instead of the man he had been expecting.

Perhaps there was something about her that had worked its way past his normal defences so that he had failed to go down the predicted route.

'I'm happy to sign whatever silence clause you want.

One word of what we've spoken about here, and you will have my full permission to fling me into jail and throw away the key.'

'I thought you said that you weren't melodramatic.'

'I'm insulted that you think I'd break the confidence you have in me to do my job and keep the details of it to myself.'

'You may be insulted, but are you surprised?' He rose to his feet, towering over her, and she fell back a couple of steps and held onto the back of the kitchen chair.

Alessio, on his way to make them some coffee, sensed the change in the atmosphere the way a big cat can sense the presence of prey in the shift of the wind. Their eyes met and something inside him, something that operated on an instinctual level, understood that, however scathing and derisive her tone of voice had been, she was tuned in to him in ways that matched his.

Tuned in to him in ways that were sexual.

The realisation struck him from out of nowhere and yet, as he held her gaze a few seconds longer than was necessary, he actually doubted himself because her expression was so tight, straightforward and openly annoyed.

'I am a man who is accustomed to taking precautions,' he murmured huskily.

'I get that.' Especially after everything he had told her. Of course he would want to make sure that he didn't leave himself open to exploitation of any kind. That was probably one of the rules by which he lived his life.

So he was right; why should she be surprised that he had taken her to task?

Except she had been lulled into a false sense of confidences shared, had warmed to the fact that he had opened up to her, and in the process had chosen to ignore the reality, which was that he had decided that he had no choice. He hadn't opened up to her because she was special. He had opened up to her because it was necessary to make her task a little easier.

'Do you?'

'Of course I do,' she said on a sigh. 'I'm just not used to people distrusting me. I'm one of the most reliable people I know when it comes to keeping a secret.'

'Really?' Mere inches separated them. He could feel the warmth radiating from her body out towards his and he wondered again whether his instincts had been right when they had told him that she was not as unaffected by him as she would have liked to pretend.

'Yes!' She relaxed with a laugh. 'When I was a teenager, I was the one person all the lads turned to when it came to confidences. They knew I would never breathe a word when they told me that they fancied someone, or asked me what I thought it would take to impress someone else…'

And all the while, Alessio thought to himself, you were taking lessons in self-defence.

Never one to do much prying into female motivations, he was surprised to find that he quite wanted to know more about her. 'You've won your argument,' he said with a slow smile.

'You mean, you won't be asking me to sign something?'

'No. So there will be no need for you to live in fear that you will be flung into prison and the key thrown away if the mood takes me.' His eyes dipped down to the barely visible swell of her small breasts under the baggy tee-shirt.

'I appreciate that,' Lesley told him sincerely. 'I don't know how easy I would have found it, working for someone who didn't trust me. So I shall start first thing in the morning.' She suddenly realised just how close their bodies were to one another and she shuffled a couple of discreet inches back. 'If it's all the same to you, you can point me in the direction of your computer and I'll spend the morning there, and the afternoon going through your daughter's rooms just in case I find anything of interest. And you needn't worry about asking your housekeeper to prepare any lunch for me. I usually just eat on the run. I can fill you in when you return from London or else I can call you if you decide to stay in London overnight.'

Alessio inclined his head in agreeable assent—except, maybe there would be no need for that.

Maybe he would stay here in the country—so much more restful than London and so much easier were he to be at hand.

CHAPTER FOUR

LESLEY WAS NOT finding life particularly restful. Having been under the impression that Alessio would be commuting to and from London, with a high possibility of remaining in London for at least part of the time, she'd been dismayed when, two days previously, he'd informed her that there had been a change of plan.

'I'll be staying here,' he had said the morning after she had arrived. 'Makes sense.'

Lesley had no idea how he had reached that conclusion. How did it make sense for him to be around: bothering her; getting under her skin; just *being* within her line of vision and therefore compelling her to look at him?

'You'll probably have a lot of questions and it'll be easier if I'm here to answer them.'

'I could always phone you,' she had said, staring at him with rising panic, because she'd been able to see just how the week was going to play out.

'And then,' he had continued, steamrollering over her interruption, 'I would feel guilty were I to leave you here on your own. The house is very big. My conscience wouldn't be able to live with the thought that you might find it quite unsettling being here with no one around.'

He had directed her to where she would be working

and she'd been appalled to find that she would be sharing office space with him.

'Of course, if you find it uncomfortable working in such close proximity to me, then naturally I can set up camp somewhere else. The house has enough rooms to accommodate one of them being turned into a makeshift work place.'

She had closed her mouth and said nothing, because what had there been to say? That, yes, she *would* find it uncomfortable working in such close proximity to him, because she was just too *aware* of him for her own good; because he made her nervous and tense; because her skin tingled the second he got too close?

She had moved from acknowledging that the man was sexy to accepting that she was attracted to him. She had no idea how that could be the case, given that he just wasn't the sort of person she had ever envisaged herself taking an interest in, but she had given up fighting it. There was just something too demanding about his physicality for her to ignore.

So she had spent her mornings in a state of rigid, hyper-sensitive awareness. She had been conscious of his every small move as he'd peered at his computer screen, reached across his desk to get something or swivelled his chair so that he could find a more comfortable position for his long legs.

She had not been able to block out the timbre of his deep voice whenever he was on the phone. She wouldn't have been able to recall any of the conversations he had had, but she could recall exactly what that voice did to her.

The range of unwanted physical sensations he evoked in her was frankly exhausting.

So she had contrived to have a simple routine of disappearing outside to communicate with her office on the pretext that she didn't want to disturb him.

Besides, she had added, making sure to forestall any objections, she never got the chance to leave London. She had never been to stay at a country estate in her life before. It would be marvellous if she could take advantage of the wonderful opportunity he had given her by working outdoors so that she could enjoy being in the countryside, especially given that the weather was so brilliant.

He had acquiesced although when he had looked at her she had been sure that she could detect a certain amount of amusement.

Now, in a break with this routine, Lesley had decided to start on Rachel's rooms.

She had gone over all of the emails with a fine toothcomb and had found no evidence that the mystery writer was aware of Bianca's past.

She looked around room number one and wondered where to begin.

As per specific instructions, Violet had left everything as it was and Lesley, by no means a neat freak, was not looking forward to going through the stacks of dispersed clothes, books, magazines and random bits of paper that littered the ground.

But she dug in, working her way steadily through the chaos, flinging clothes in the stainless-steel hamper she had dragged from the massive bathroom and marvelling that a child of sixteen could possess so much designer clothing.

This was what money bought: expensive clothes and jewellery. But no amount of expensive clothes and jewellery could fix a broken relationship and, over the past two days, she had seen for herself just how broken the relationship between father and daughter was.

He kept his emotions under tight control but every so often there were glimpses of the man underneath who was confused at his inability to communicate with his daughter and despairing of what the future held for them.

And yet, he wanted to protect her, and would do anything to that end.

She began rifling through the pockets of a pair of jeans, her mind playing with the memory of just how weirdly close the past couple of days had brought them.

Or, at least, *her*.

But then, she thought ruefully, she was handicapped by the fact that she found him attractive. She was therefore primed to analyse everything he said, to be super-attentive to every stray remark, to hang onto his every word with breathless intensity.

Thank God he didn't know what was going through her head.

It took her a couple of seconds before the piece of paper she extracted from the jeans pocket made sense and then a couple more seconds before the links she had begun to see in the emails began to tie up in front of her.

More carefully now, she began feeling her way through the mess, inspecting everything in her path. She went over the clothes she had carelessly chucked into the hamper just in case she had missed something.

Had she expected to find anything at all like this, searching through a few rooms? No; maybe when she got to the computer or the tablet, or whatever other computer gadgets might be lying around.

But scribbles on a bit of paper? No. She thought that teenagers were way beyond using pens and paper by way of communication.

What else might she find?

She had lost that initial feeling of intruding in someone else's space. Something about the messiness made her search more acceptable.

No attempts had been made to hide anything and nothing was under lock and key.

Did that make a difference? In a strange way it did, as did the little things lying about that showed Rachel for the child she still was, even if she had entered the teenage battleground of rebellion and disobedience.

Her art book was wonderful. There were cute little doodles in the margins of her exercise books. Her stationery was very cute, with lots of puppy motifs on the pencil cases and folders. It was at odds with the rest of what was to be found in the room.

An hour and a half into the search, Lesley opened the first of the wardrobes and gasped at the racks of clothes confronting her.

You didn't need to be a connoisseur of fine clothing to know that these were the finest money could buy. She ran her hands through the dresses, skirts and tops and felt silk, cashmere and pure cotton. Some of them were youthful and brightly coloured, others looked far too grown-up for a sixteen-year-old child. Quite a few things still had tags attached because they had yet to be used.

As she pushed the clothes at the front aside, she came across some dresses at the back that were clearly too old for a sixteen-year-old; they must have belonged to Rachel's mother. Lesley gently pulled a demure black dress from the selection and admired the fine material and elegant cut of the design. She knew that it was wrong to try on someone else's clothes but she lost her head for a moment and suddenly found herself slipping into the gorgeous creation. As she turned to look at herself in the mirror, she gasped.

Usually she was awkward, one of the lads, at her most comfortable when she was exchanging banter; yet the creature staring back at her wasn't that person at all. The creature staring back at her was a leggy, attractive young woman with a good figure, good legs and a long neck.

She spun away from the mirror suddenly as she heard the door open and saw Alessio look at her in shock.

'What are you doing here?' She felt naked as his eyes slowly raked over her, from the top of her head, along her body and then all the way back again.

Alessio couldn't stop looking at her. He had left the office to stretch his legs and had decided to check on how Lesley's search was coming along. He hadn't expected to find her in a stunning cocktail dress, her legs seeming to go on for ever.

'Well?' Lesley folded her arms defensively, although what she really wanted to do was somehow reach down and cover her exposed thighs. The skirt should have been a couple of inches above the knee but, because she was obviously taller than Rachel's mother had been, it was obscenely short on her.

'I've interrupted a catwalk session,' he murmured, walking slowly towards her. 'My apologies.'

'I was… I thought…'

'It suits you, just in case you're interested in what I think. The dress, I mean. You should reveal your legs more often.'

'If you would please just go, I'll get changed. I apologise for having tried on the dress. It was totally out of order, and if you want to give me my marching orders then I would completely understand.' She had never felt so mortified in her entire life. What must he be thinking? She had taken something that didn't belong to her and put it on, an especially unforgivable offence, considering she was under his roof in the capacity of a paid employee.

His 'catwalk' comment struck her as an offensive insult but there was no way she was going to call him out on that. She just wanted him to leave the room but he showed no signs of going.

'Why would I give you your marching orders?' She was bright red and as stiff as a plank of wood.

Any other woman would have been overjoyed to be the centre of his attention, as she now was, but instead she was staring straight ahead, unblinking, doing her utmost to shut him out of her line of vision.

He had never wanted a woman as much as he wanted this one right now. Mind and body fused. This wasn't just another of his glamorous, sex-kitten women. This thinking, questioning, irreverent creature was in a different league.

The attraction he had felt for her, which had been there from the second they had met, clarified into the absolute certainty that he wanted her in his bed. It was a thought he had flirted with, dwelled on; rejected because she'd challenged him on too many levels and he liked his women unchallenging.

But, hell…

'Please leave.'

'You don't have to take off the dress,' he said in a lazy drawl. 'I'd quite like to see you working in that outfit.'

'You're making fun of me and I don't like it.' She had managed to blank him out, so that she was just aware of him on the periphery of her vision, but she could still feel his power radiating outwards, wrapping around her like something thick, suffocating and tangible.

She felt like something small and helpless being circled by a beautiful, dangerous predator.

Except he would never hurt her. No; his capacity for destruction lay in his ability to make her hurt herself by believing what he was saying, by allowing her feelings for him get the better of her. She had never realised that lust could be so overwhelming. Nothing had prepared her for the crazy, inappropriate emotions that rode roughshod over her prized and treasured common sense.

'I'll pretend I didn't hear that,' Alessio said softly. Then he reached out and ran his hand along her arm, feeling its soft, silky smoothness. She was so slender. For a few seconds, Lesley didn't react, then the feel of his warm hand on her skin made her stumble backwards with a yelp.

His instincts had been right. How could he have doubted himself? The electricity between them flowed both ways. He stepped back and looked at her lazily. Her eyes were huge and she looked very young and very vulnerable. And she was still wobbling in the high stilettos; that was how uncomfortable she was in a pair of heels. He was struck with a pressing desire to see her dolled up to the nines and, with an even more contradictory one, to have her naked in his arms.

'I'll leave you to get back into your clothes,' he said with the gentleness of someone trying to calm a panicked, highly strung thoroughbred. 'And, to answer your question as to what I'm doing here, I thought I would just pop in and see if your search up here was being fruitful.'

Relieved to have the focus off her and onto work, Lesley allowed some of the tension to ooze out of her body.

'I *have* found one or two things you might be interested in,' she said with staccato jerkiness. 'And I'll come right down to the office.'

'Better still, meet me outside. I'll get Violet to bring us out some tea.' He smiled, encouraging her to relax further. It was all he could do not to let his eyes wander over her, drink her in. He lowered his eyes and reluctantly spun round, walking towards the door and knowing that she wouldn't move a muscle until he was well and truly out of the suite of rooms and heading down the staircase.

Once outside, he couldn't wait for her to join him. He was oblivious to his surroundings as he stared off into the distance, thinking of how she had looked in that outfit. She had incredible legs, an incredible body and it was all the more enhanced by the fact that she was so unaware of her charms.

Five brothers; no mother; karate lessons when the rest of her friends were practising the feminine skills that would serve them well in later life. Was that why she was so skittish around him? Was she skittish around *all* men, or was it just him? Was that why she chose to dress the way she did, why she projected such a capable image, why she deliberately seemed to spurn feminine clothes?

He found himself idly trying to work out what made her tick and he was enjoying the game when he saw her walking towards him with a sheaf of papers in her hand, all business as usual.

'Thank you.' Lesley sat down, taking the glass that was offered to her. She had been so hot and bothered after he had left that she had taken time out to wash her face in cold water and gather herself. 'First of all—and I'm almost one-hundred-per-cent sure about this—our emailing friend has no idea about your wife or the sort of person she was.'

Alessio leant closer, forearms resting on his thighs. 'And you've reached that conclusion because…?'

'Because I've been through each and every email very carefully, looking for clues. I've also found a couple of earlier emails which arrived in your junk box and for some reason weren't deleted. They weren't significant. Perhaps our friend was just having a bit of fun.'

'So you think this isn't about a blackmail plot to do with revelations about Bianca?'

'Yes, partly from reading through the emails and partly common sense. I think if they involved your ex-wife there would have been some sort of guarded reference made that would have warned you of what was to come. And, whilst he or she knew what they were doing and were careful to leave as few tracks behind them as they could, some of those emails are definitely more rushed than others.'

'Woman's intuition?' There was genuine curiosity in his voice and Lesley nodded slowly.

'I think so. What's really significant, though, is that the Internet cafés used were all in roughly the same area, within a radius of a dozen miles or so, and they are all in the general vicinity of where Rachel goes to school. Which leads me to think that she is at the centre of this in some way, shape or form because the person responsible probably knows her or knows of her.'

Alessio sat back and rubbed his eyes wearily. Lesley could see the strain visible beneath the cool, collected exterior when he next looked at her. He might have approached this problem with pragmatism and detachment, as a job to be done—but his daughter was involved and that showed on his face now, in the worry and the stress.

'Any idea of what could be going on? It could still

be that our friend, as you call him, has information on Bianca and wants me to pay him for not sharing that information with Rachel.'

'Does Rachel know anything about what her mother was like as…err…a young girl? I mean, when she was still married to you? I know your daughter would have been a toddler with no memories of that time, but you know how it is: overheard conversations between adults, bits and pieces of gossip from friends or family or whatever.'

Alessio leaned back in the chair and closed his eyes.

'As far as I am aware, Rachel is completely in the dark about Bianca, but who knows? We haven't talked about it. We've barely got past the stage of polite pleasantries.'

Lesley stared at his averted profile. Seeing them in repose, as now, she felt the full impact of his devastating good looks. His sensual mouth lost its stern contours; she could appreciate the length and thickness of his eyelashes, the strong angle of his jaw, the tousled blackness of his slightly too-long hair. His fingers were linked loosely on his stomach; she took in the dark hair on his forearms and then burned when she wondered where that dark hair was replicated.

She wondered whether she should tell him about those random scribbles she had found and decided against it. They formed part of the jigsaw puzzle but she would hang on until more of the pieces came together. It was only fair. He was a desperately concerned father, worried about a daughter he barely knew; to add yet more stress to his situation, when she wasn't even one-hundred per cent sure whether what she had found would prove significant in the end, seemed downright selfish.

The lingering embarrassment she had brought with her after the mini-skirt-wearing episode faded as the silence lengthened between them, a telling indication of his state of mind.

It would have cost him dearly to confide the personal details of his situation with his ex-wife. No matter that he had been practically a child at the time. No one enjoyed being used and Alessio, in particular, was a proud man today and would have been a proud boy all those years ago.

Her heart softened and she resisted the temptation to reach out and stroke the side of his cheek.

'I'm making you feel awkward,' Alessio murmured, breaking the silence, but not opening his eyes or turning in her direction.

Lesley buried the wickedly tantalising thought of touching his cheek. 'Of course not!'

'I don't suppose you banked on this sort of situation when you agreed to the job.'

'I don't suppose you banked on it either when you decided to hire me.'

'True,' he admitted with a ghost of a smile. 'So, where do you suggest we go from here? Quiz Rachel when she gets home day after tomorrow? Try and find out if she has any idea what's going on?' He listened as she ran through some options. He liked hearing her talk. He liked the soft but decisive tone of her voice. He liked the way she could talk to him like this, on his level, with no coy intonations and no irritating indications that she wanted the conversation to take any personal detours.

Mind you, she had so much information about him that personal detours were pretty much an irrelevance:

there really weren't that many nooks and crannies left to discover.

His mind swung back to when he had caught her wearing that dress and his body began to stir into life.

'Talk to me about something else,' he ordered huskily when there was a pause in the conversation. This was as close to relaxation he had come in a long time, despite the grim nature of what was going on. He had his eyes closed, the sun was on his face and his body felt lazy and nicely lethargic.

'What do you want me to talk about?' She could understand why he might not want to dwell ad infinitum on a painful subject, even one that needed to be discussed.

'You. I want you to talk about you.'

Even though he wasn't looking at her, Lesley still reddened. That voice of his; had he any idea how sexy it was? No, of course not.

'I'm a very boring person,' she half-laughed with embarrassment. 'Besides, you know all the basic stuff: my brothers; my dad bringing us all up on his own.'

'So let's skip the basics. Tell me what drove you to try on that dress.'

'I don't want to talk about that.' Lesley's skin prickled with acute discomfort. The mortification she had felt assailed her all over again and she clenched her fists on her lap. 'I've already apologised and I'd really rather we drop the subject and pretend it never happened. It was a mistake.'

'You're embarrassed.'

'Of course I am.'

'No need to be, and I'm not prying. I'm really just trying to grasp anything that might take my mind off what's happening right now with Rachel.'

Suddenly Lesley felt herself deflate. While she was on her high horse, defending her position and beating back his very natural curiosity, he was in the unenviable position of having had to open the door to his past and let her in.

Was it any wonder that he was desperate to take his mind off his situation? Talking relentlessly about something worrying only magnified the worry and anxiety.

'I—I don't know why I tried it,' Lesley offered haltingly. 'Actually, I do know why I tried it on. I was never one for dresses and frocks when I was a teenager. That was stuff meant for other girls but not for me.'

'Because you lacked a mother's guiding hand,' Alessio contributed astutely. 'And even more influential was the fact that you had five brothers.' He grinned and some of the worry that had been etched on his face lifted. 'I remember what I was like and what my friends were like when we were fourteen—not sensitive. I bet they gave you a hard time.'

Lesley laughed. 'And the rest of it. At any rate, I had one embarrassing encounter with a mini-skirt and I decided after that that I was probably better off not going down that road. Besides, at the age of fourteen I was already taller than all the other girls in my class. Downplaying my height didn't involve wearing dresses and short skirts.'

Alessio slowly opened his eyes and then inclined his head so that he was looking directly at her.

Her skin was like satin. As far as he knew, she had yet to make use of the swimming pool, but sitting outside for the past couple of afternoons in the blazing sun had lent a golden tint to her complexion. It suited her.

'But you're not fourteen any longer,' he said huskily.

Lesley was lost for words. Drowning in his eyes, her

throat suddenly went dry and her body turned to lead. She couldn't move a muscle. She could just watch him, watching her.

He would physically have to get out of his chair if he were to come any closer, and he made no move to do anything of the sort, but she was still overwhelmed by the feeling that he was going to kiss her. It was written in the dark depths of his eyes, a certain intent that made her quiver and tremble inside.

'No, I don't suppose I am,' she choked out.

'But you still don't wear short skirts…'

'Old habits die hard.' She gave up trying to look away. She didn't care what he thought—not at this moment in time, at any rate. 'I… There's no need to dress up for the sort of job that I do. Jeans and jumpers are what we all wear.'

'You don't do justice to your body.' He glanced at his watch. He had broken off working in part, as he had said, to check on Lesley and see whether she had managed to find anything in Rachel's quarters; but also in part because he was due in London for a meeting.

The time had run away. It was much later than he had imagined…something about the sun, the slight breeze, the company of the woman sitting next to him, the way she had frozen to the spot… He wondered whether any man had ever complimented her about the way she looked or whether she had spent a lifetime assuming that no one would, therefore making sure that she carved her own niche through her intelligence and ambition.

He wondered what she would do if he touched her, kissed her.

More than ever, he wanted to have her. In fact, he was tempted to abandon the meeting in London and spend the rest of this lazy afternoon playing the game of seduction.

Already she was standing up, all of a fluster, telling him that she was feeling a little hot and wanted to get back into the shade. With an inward, rueful sigh of resignation, he followed suit.

'You're doing a brilliant job, trying to unravel what the hell is going on with these emails,' he said, uncomfortably aware of his body demanding a certain type of attention that was probably going to make his drive down to London a bit uncomfortable.

Lesley put some much-needed physical distance between them.

What had happened just then? He seemed normal enough now. Had it been her imagination playing tricks on her, making her think that he was going to kiss her? Or was it her own forbidden attraction trying to find a way to become a reality?

It absolutely terrified her that she might encourage him to think that she was attracted to him. It was even more terrifying that she might be reading all sorts of nonsense into his throwaway remarks. The guy was the last word in eligible. He was charming, highly intelligent and sophisticated, and he probably had that sexy, ever so slightly flirty manner with every woman he spoke to. It was just the kind of person he was and misinterpreting anything he said in her favour would be something she did at her own peril.

'Thank you. You're paying me handsomely to do just that.'

Alessio frowned. He didn't like money being brought into the conversation. It lowered the tone.

'Well, carry on the good work,' he said with equal politeness. 'And you'll have the house all to yourself until tomorrow to do it. I have an important meeting in London and I'll be spending the night there in my apartment.' He scowled at her immediate look of relief. Hell, she was attracted to him, but she was determined to fight it, despite the clear signals he had sent that the feeling was reciprocated. Didn't she know that for a man like him, a man who could snap his fingers and have any woman he wanted, her reticence was a challenge?

And yet, was he the type to set off in pursuit of someone who was reluctant—even though she might be as hot for him as he was for her?

A night away might cool him down a bit.

He left her dithering in the hall, seeing him off, but with a look of impatience on her face for him to be gone.

She needed this. Her nerves were getting progressively more shot by the minute; she couldn't wait for him to leave. She went to see him off, half-expecting him suddenly to decide that he wasn't going anywhere after all, and sagged with relief when the front door slammed behind him and she heard the roar of his car diminishing as he cleared the courtyard and disappeared down the long drive.

She couldn't stay. Certainly, she wanted to be out by the time his daughter arrived. She just couldn't bear the tension of being around him: she couldn't bear the loss of self-control, the way her eyes wanted to seek him out, the constant roller-coaster ride of her emotions. She felt vulnerable and confused.

Well, she had found rather more searching through Rachel's room than she had told him. Not quite enough, but just a little bit more information and she would have sufficient to present to him and leave with the case closed.

She had seen the desk-top computer and was sure

that there would be a certain amount of helpful information there.

She had an afternoon, a night and hopefully part of the day tomorrow, and during that time she would make sure that everything was sorted, because she desperately needed to return to the safety of her comfort zone…

CHAPTER FIVE

LESLEY FLEXED HER fingers, which were stiff from working solidly on Rachel's desk-top for the past two and a half hours.

Alessio had given her the green light to look through anything and everything in his daughter's room and she knew that he was right to allow her to do so. If Rachel was under some sort of threat, whatever that threat was, then everything had to be done to neutralise the situation, even if it meant an invasion of her privacy.

However, Lesley had still felt guilty and nervous when she had sat down in front of the computer to begin opening files.

She had expected to find lots of personal teenage stuff. She had never been one of those girls who had sat around giggling and pouring her heart out to all her friends. She and her friends had mostly belonged to the sporting set, and the sporting set had only occasionally crossed over into the cheerleader set, which was where most of the giggling about boys and confiding had taken place.

However, the computer seemed largely to store school work. Lesley had assumed that the more personal information was probably carried on Rachel's tablet, or else her mobile phone, neither of which were in the house.

But she had found a couple of little strands that added to the building jigsaw puzzle.

Most of the really important information, however, had been gathered the old-fashioned way: pockets of jeans; scraps of paper; old exercise books; margins of text books; letters tossed carelessly in the drawer by the bed.

There had been no attempt to hide any of the stuff Lesley had gathered, and that made her feel much better.

Rachel might have given orders to a very pliant housekeeper not to go anywhere near her rooms, but had there been a little part of her that maybe wanted the information to be found? Was that why she had not destroyed notes that were definitely incriminating?

Lesley could only speculate.

By six that evening, she was exhausted. She ached all over, but she knew that she would be able to hand everything she had found over to Alessio and be on her way.

She felt a little panicky when she thought about getting into her little car and driving away from him for ever, then she told herself that it was just as well she was going to do that, because panicking at the prospect of not seeing him was a very dangerous place to be.

How had he managed to get under her skin so thoroughly and so fast?

When it came to men, she was a girl who had always taken things slowly. Friendships were built over a reasonable period of time. Generally speaking, during that protracted build-up any prospect of the friendship developing into something more serious was apt to fizzle out, which always reassured her that the relationship had not been destined.

But the speed with which Alessio had succeeded in filling her head was scary.

She found that even being alone in his house for a few hours was an unsettling business because she missed his presence!

In the space of only a couple of days, she had become accustomed to living life in the emotional fast lane; had become used to a heightened state of awareness, knowing that he was *around.* When she sat outside in the garden—working on her lap-top, enjoying the peace of the countryside, telling herself what a relief it was that she was not in the same room as him—she was still *conscious* of the fact that he was in the house. Somewhere.

With a little sigh of frustration, she decided that she would have a swim.

She hadn't been near the pool since she had arrived. She hadn't been able to deal with the prospect of him suggesting that he join her, even less with the prospect of him seeing just how angular, flat-chested and boyish her figure was.

He might have made the occasional flirty remark, but she had seen the sort of women he was attracted to. He had handed over his computer files to her and within them were photos of him with various busty, curvaceous, five-foot-two blonde bombshells. They all looked like clones of Marilyn Monroe.

But he wasn't here now, and it was still so hot and muggy, even at this hour of the evening.

When she looked at herself in the mirror, she was startled at how much it changed her appearance. However, she had seen herself in her navy-blue bikini sufficient times to be reassured that she was the same lanky Lesley she had always been.

Without bothering to glance at her reflection, she grabbed a towel from the bathroom and headed downstairs for the pool.

She should have felt wary venturing out with no one around, and just acres upon acres of fields and open land stretching away into the distance, but she didn't. In fact, she felt far more cautious in London, where she was constantly surrounded by people and where there was no such thing as complete darkness even in the dead of night in the middle of winter.

She dived cleanly into the water, gasping at the temperature, but then her body acclimatised as she began swimming.

She was a good swimmer. After being cooped up in front of a computer for several hours, it felt good to be exercising, and she swam without stopping, cutting through the water length after length after length.

She wasn't sure exactly how long she swam; maybe forty-five minutes. She could feel the beginning of that pleasant burn in her body that indicated that her muscles were being stretched to their limit.

At this point, she pulled herself up out of the pool, water sluicing down her body, her short, dark hair plastered down…and it was only then that she noticed Alessio standing to one side, half-concealed in the shadow of one of the trees fringing the side of the veranda.

It took a few seconds for her brain to register his presence there at all because she hadn't been expecting him.

And it took a few seconds more for her to realise that, not only was he standing there, but she wasn't even sure how long he had been standing there looking at her.

With an outraged yelp she walked quickly over to where she had dumped her towel on one of the chairs by the pool and, by the time she had secured it around her, he had walked lazily to where she was standing.

'I hope I didn't interrupt your workout,' he murmured without a hint of an apology in his voice.

'You're not supposed to be here!'

'There was a slight change of plan.'

'You should have warned me that you were going to be coming back!'

'I didn't think I needed to inform you that I would be returning to my own home.'

'How long have you been standing there?' She couldn't bring herself to meet those amused dark eyes. She was horribly conscious of what she must look like, with her wet hair like a cap on her head and her face completely bare of make-up—not that she ever wore much, but still.

'Long enough to realise that it's been a while since I used that pool. In fact, I can't remember the last time I stepped foot in it.' Water droplets were like tiny diamonds on her eyelashes and he wished she would look at him so that he could read the expression in her eyes. Was she genuinely annoyed that he had disturbed her, shown up unexpectedly? Or was she all of a dither because she had been caught off-guard, because he was seeing her for the first time without her armour of jeans, flats and faded tee-shirts? Clothes that neutralised her femininity.

He wondered what she would say if he told her just how delicious she looked, standing there dripping wet with only a towel that barely covered her.

He also wondered what she would say if he told her that he had been standing there for the better part of fifteen minutes, mesmerised as he'd watched her swimming, as at home in the water as a seal. He had been so wrapped up in the sight that he had completely forgotten why he had been obliged to drive back from London.

'Wait right here,' he urged suddenly. 'I'm going to join you. Give me ten minutes. It'll do me good to get rid of the London grime.'

'Join me?' Lesley was frankly horrified.

'You don't have a problem with that, do you?'

'No…err…'

'Good. I'll be back before you can get back in the water.'

Lesley was frozen to the spot as she watched him disappear back through the sprawling triple-fronted French doors that led into the conservatory.

Then, galvanised into action—because diving in while he watched was just out of the question—she hurried back into the water. What choice did she have? To have told him that she was fed up swimming and wanted to go inside, just as he was about to join her in the pool, would have been tantamount to confessing just how awkward he made her feel. The last thing she wanted was for him to know the effect he had on her. He might have some idea that she wasn't as impartial to his presence as she liked to pretend but her feelings were more confused than that and ran a lot deeper.

That was something she was desperate to keep to herself. She could just about cope if he thought that she fancied him; half the female population in the country between the ages of eighteen and eighty would have fancied the man, so it would be no big deal were he to include her in that category.

But it was more than that. Not only was she not the type to randomly fancy guys because of the way they looked, but her reactions to him pointed to something a lot more complex than a simple case of lust which could easily be cured by putting some distance between them.

She had just reached the shallow end of the pool

when Alessio emerged back out in the mellow evening sunshine.

Lesley thought that she might faint. Only now did she fully comprehend how much time she had spent daydreaming about him, about what he might look like under those expensive, casual designer clothes he was fond of wearing.

What would his body look like?

Now she knew: lean, bronzed and utterly beautiful. His shoulders were broad and muscled and his torso tapered to a narrow waist and hips.

He was at home with his body, that much was evident from the way he moved with an easy, casual grace.

Lesley sat on one of the steps at the shallow end of the pool, so that she was levered into a half-sitting position on her elbows while her long legs and most of her body remained under the surface of the water. She felt safer that way.

He dived into the water, as straight as an arrow, and swam steadily and powerfully towards her. It took every ounce of will power not to flinch back as he reared up out of the water and joined her on the step.

'Nice,' he said appreciatively, wiping his face with the palm of his hand, then leaning back just as she did.

'You haven't explained what you're doing here.' Lesley eyed the proximity of his body nervously.

'And I shall do that as soon as we're inside. For the moment, I just want to enjoy being out here. I don't get much by way of time out. I don't want to spoil it by launching into the unexpected little problem that's cropped up.' He glanced across to her. 'You're a good swimmer.'

'Thank you.'

'Been swimming a long time?'

'Since I was four.' She paused and then continued, because talking seemed a bit less stressful than remaining silent and concentrating all her energies on what he was doing to her. 'My father had always been a good swimmer. All my brothers were as well. After my mother died, he got it into his head that he would channel all his energy into getting me into competitive swimming. The boys were all a bit older and had their own hobbies, but he's fond of telling me that I was fertile ground for him to work on.' Lesley laughed and relaxed a little. 'So he made sure to take me down to the local swimming baths at least twice a week. I was out of arm bands and swimming by the time I was five.'

'But you didn't end up becoming a professional swimmer.'

'I didn't,' Lesley admitted. 'Although I entered lots of competitions right up until I went to secondary school, then once I was in secondary school I began to play lots of different types of sport and the swimming was put on the back burner.'

'What sport did you play?' Alessio thought of his last girlfriend, whose only stab at anything energetic had involved the ski slope. He had once made the mistake of trying to get her to play a game of squash with him and had been irritated when she had shrieked with horror at the thought of getting too sweaty. Her hair, apparently, would not have been able to cope. He wondered whether she would have submerged herself in the pool the way Lesley had or whether she would have spent her time lying on a sun lounger and only dipping her feet in when the heat became unbearable.

Any wonder he had broken up with her after a couple of months?

'Squash, tennis, hockey, and of course in between I had my self-defence classes.'

'Energetic.'

'Very.'

'And in between all of that vigorous exercise you still had time for studying.'

Hence no time at all for what every other teenage girl would have been doing. Lesley read behind that mild observation. 'How else would I have ever been able to have a career?' Lesley responded tartly. 'Playing sport is all well and good but it doesn't get you jobs at the end of the day.' She stood up. 'I've been out here for long enough. I should really get back inside, have a shower. Please don't let me keep you from enjoying the pool. It's a shame to have this and not make use of it, especially when you think that it's so rare for the weather to be as good as it has been recently.' She didn't give him time to answer. Instead, she headed for her towel and breathed a sigh of relief when she had wrapped it around her.

When she turned around, it was to find him standing so close to her that she gave a little stumble back, almost crashing into the sun lounger behind her.

'Steady.' Alessio reached out and gripped her arms, then left his hands on her arms. 'I should really talk to you about what's brought me back here. I've got quite a bit of work to catch up on and I'll probably work through the night.'

Lesley found that she couldn't focus on anything while he was still holding her.

'Of course,' she eventually managed to croak. 'I'll go and have a shower, and then shall I meet you in the office?' She could smell him—the clean, chlorinated scent of the swimming pool combined with the heady aroma of the sun drying him as he stood there, practically naked.

'Meet me in the kitchen instead.' Alessio released her abruptly. Just then every instinct inside him wanted to pull her towards him and kiss her, taste her, see whether she would be as delectable as his imagination told him she would be. The intensity of what had shot through him was disturbing.

'I…I didn't expect you to return; I told Violet that there was no need to prepare anything for me before she left. In fact, I let her go early. I do hope you don't mind but I'm accustomed to cooking for myself. I was only going to do myself a plate of pasta.'

'Sounds good to me.'

'Right, then,' Lesley said faintly. She pushed her fingers through her hair, spiking it up.

She left him watching her and dashed upstairs for a very quick shower.

She should have found his unexpected arrival intensely annoying. It had thrown her whole evening out of sync. But there was a dark excitement swirling around inside her and she found that she was looking forward to having dinner with him, stupidly thrilled that he was back at the house.

She told herself that it was simply because she would be able to fill him in on all sorts of discoveries she had made and, the faster she filled him in, the sooner she would be able to leave and the quicker her life would return to normal. Normality seemed like a lifetime away.

He wasn't in the kitchen when she got there half an hour later, with all her paperwork in a folder, so she poured herself a glass of wine and waited for him.

She couldn't think what might have brought him back to his country estate. Something to do with his daughter, she was sure, but what? Might he have discovered something independently? Something that would make it easier for her to tell him what she thought this whole situation was about?

He strolled in when she was halfway through her glass of wine and proceeded to pour himself a whisky and soda.

'I need this,' Alessio said heavily, sinking onto the chair at the head of the table and angling it so that he could stretch his legs out whilst still facing her. 'My mother-in-law called when I was in the middle of my meetings.'

'Is that unusual?'

'Extremely. We may well be on cordial terms but not so cordial that she telephones out of the blue. There's still that ugly residue of their manipulation, although I will concede that Bianca's mother was not the one behind it. And it has to be said that, for the duration of our divorce, it was only thanks to Claudia that I ever got to see Rachel at all. I can count the number of times that happened on the fingers of one hand, but then Claudia never was a match for her daughter.' He caught himself in the act of wanting to talk more about the destructive marriage that had made him the cynical man he was today. How had that happened?

'What did she want?' Lesley eventually asked.

'Rachel has been staying with her for the past four weeks. Pretty much as soon as her school ended, she decided that she wanted to go over there. She doesn't know a great deal of people around here and only a handful in London. The down side of a boarding school out in the country, I suppose.' He sighed heavily and tipped the remainder of his drink down before resting the empty glass on the table and staring at it in brooding silence.

'Yes,' Lesley contributed vaguely. 'It must be difficult.'

'At any rate, the upshot appears to be that my daughter is refusing to return to the UK.'

Lesley's mouth fell open and Alessio smiled crookedly at her. 'She's refusing to speak to me on the telephone. She's dug her heels in and has decided to set up camp with Claudia and, Claudia being Claudia, she lacks the strength to stand up to my daughter.'

'You must be a little put out.'

'That's the understatement of the hour.' He stood up and signalled to her that they should start preparing something to eat. He needed to move around. For a small window, he had been so preoccupied with her, with arriving back and surprising her in the swimming pool, that he had actually put the gravity of the situation to the back of his mind, but now it had returned in full force.

Strangely, he was thankful that Lesley was there.

As if knowing that he would return to the topic in his own time, Lesley began preparing their meal. She had earlier piled all the ingredients she would need on the counter and now she began chopping mushrooms, tomatoes, onions and garlic.

For once, his silence didn't send her into instant meltdown. Rather, she began chatting easily and pleasantly. She told him about her lack of cooking experience. She joked that her brothers were all better cooks than she was and that two of them had even offered to show her the basics. She could sense him begin to unwind, even though she wasn't looking at him at all and he wasn't saying anything, just listening to her rabbit on aimlessly about nothing in particular.

It was soothing, Alessio thought as he watched her

prepare the vegetables slowly and with the painstaking care of someone who wasn't comfortable in the arena of the kitchen.

Nor was he feeling trapped at the thought of a woman busying herself in his kitchen. He cleared as she cooked. It was a picture-perfect snapshot of just the sort of domesticity he avoided at all costs.

'So…' They were sitting at the kitchen table with bowls of pasta in front of them. She had maintained a steady flow of non-threatening conversation, and it had been surprisingly easy, considering she was always a bundle of nervous tension whenever she was in his presence. 'When you say that Rachel is digging her heels in and doesn't want to return to the UK, are you saying *for ever*, or just for the remainder of the summer holidays?'

'I'm saying that she's decided that she hates it over here and doesn't want to return at all.'

'And your mother-in-law can't talk her out of that?'

'Claudia has always been the pushover in the family. Between her bullying husband and Bianca, she was the one who got dragged into their plot and now, in this situation, well, it's probably a mixture of not wanting to hurt or offend her only grandchild and wanting to go down the path of least resistance.'

'So what are you going to do about that?'

'Well, there's simply no question of Rachel staying out there and going to school.' He pushed his empty plate to one side and sat back to look at her. 'I could have waited until tomorrow to come back here and tell you this but…'

'But…?' Lesley rested her chin in the palm of her hand and looked at him. The kitchen lights hadn't been switched on. It had still been bright when they had started preparing dinner, but the sun had suddenly faded, giving way to a violet twilight that cast shadows and angles across his face.

'I have a favour to ask of you.'

'What is it?' Lesley asked cautiously. She began standing to clear the table and he circled her wrist with his hand.

'Sit. Tidying can come later, or not at all. Violet will do it in the morning. I need to ask you something and I will need your undivided attention when I do so.'

She subsided back into the chair, heart beating madly.

'I want you to accompany me to Italy,' Alessio said heavily. 'It's a big ask, I know, but my fear is that, short of dragging Rachel to the plane and forcibly strapping her to the seat, she will simply refuse to listen to a word I have to say.'

'But I don't even know your daughter, Alessio!'

'If I cannot persuade my daughter to return to the UK, this will spell the end of any chance of a relationship I will ever have with her.' He rubbed his eyes wearily and then leaned back and stared blankly up at the ceiling.

Lesley's heart went out to him. Was that how it would be? Most likely. And yet…

'There's something you should see.' She stood up and went to the folder which she had brought down with her. This was the point at which she should now point out that she had gathered as much information as she could and it was up to him to do what needed to be done. In the end, it had been fiddly, but not impossible.

'You've found something?' Alessio was suddenly alert. He sat forward and pulled his chair towards her as she began smoothing out the various bits of paper she had found and the pages she had printed out over the past couple of days she had been at the house.

She had only given him a rough, skeleton idea of her findings before, not wanting to build any pictures that might be incorrect.

'I collated all of this and, well, okay, so I told you that I didn't think that this had anything to do with your wife…'

'Ex-wife.'

'Ex-wife. Well, I was right. I managed to trace our friend. He jumped around a bit, used a few different Internet cafés to cover his tracks, but the cafés, as I told you, were all in the vicinity of your daughter's school. It took a bit of time, but I eventually identified the one he used most frequently. Most importantly, though, in one of the very early emails—one of the emails you never identified as coming from him—he used his own computer. It was a little bit tougher than I thought but I got through to the identity of the person.'

Alessio was listening intently. 'You know who he is?'

'It would have been a bit more difficult to piece together conclusively if I hadn't discovered those very early emails when he'd obviously just been testing the ground. They were very innocuous, which is why he probably thought that they would have been deleted. I guess he didn't figure that they would still be uncovered and brought out of hiding.' She shoved the stack of printed emails across to Alessio and watched as he read them one by one. She had highlighted important bits, phrases, certain ways of saying things that pointed to the same writer behind them.

'You're brilliant.'

Lesley flushed with pleasure. 'I was only doing what you paid me to do.'

'So, build me the picture,' he said softly.

She did and, as she did so, she watched his expression darken and change.

'So now you pretty much have the complete story,' she finished. 'I gathered all this so that I could actually present it to you tomorrow when you returned. I was going to tell you that there's really nothing left for me to do now.'

'I still want you to come with me to Italy.'

'I can't,' Lesley said quickly, with a note of desperation in her voice.

'You've sorted all of this out, but there is still the problem of my daughter. Bringing her back over here with this information, it's going to be even more difficult.'

That was something Lesley had not taken into account when she had worked out her plan to present him with her findings and leave while common sense and her instinct for self-preservation were still intact.

'Yes, but it all remains the same. She's going to be—I can't imagine—certainly not warm and welcoming to the person who brought the whole thing to light.'

'But you have no personal axe to grind with her.' Would she come? It suddenly seemed very important that she was at his side. He was uneasily aware that there was an element of need there. How and why had that happened? He swept aside his discomfort.

'I also have my job, Alessio.' She was certain that she should be feeling horrified and indignant at his nerve in asking her to go way beyond the bounds of what she had been paid to do. Especially when she had made such a big effort to wrap everything up so that she could escape the suffocating, dangerous effect he had on her.

'You can leave that to me,' he murmured.

'Leave that to you? How do you work that one out?'

'I've just concluded a deal to buy a string of luxury boutique hotels in Italy. Failing business, mismanagement, feuding amongst the board members; that's what the trip to London was all about. I needed to be there to finalise the details with lawyers.'

'How exciting,' Lesley said politely.

'More so than you might imagine. It's the first time I shall be dabbling in the leisure industry and, naturally, I will want a comprehensive website designed.'

'You have your own people to do that.'

'They're remarkably busy at the moment. This will be a job that will definitely have to be outsourced. Not only could it be worth a great deal of money to the company lucky enough to get the job, but there's no telling how many other jobs will come in its wake.'

'Are you *coercing* me?'

'I prefer to call it *persuasion*.'

'I don't believe it.'

'I usually get what I want,' Alessio said with utter truth. 'And what I want is for you to come with me to Italy and, if this proves a helpful lever, then that's all to the good. I'm sure when I explain to your boss the size and scale of the job, and the fact that it would be extremely useful to have you over there so that you can soak up the atmosphere and get a handle on how best to pitch the project…' He gave an elegant shrug and a smile of utter devastation; both relayed the message that she was more or less trapped.

Naturally she could turn down his offer but her boss might be a little miffed should he get to hear that. They were a thriving company but, with the current economic climate, potential setbacks lurked round every corner.

Whatever work came their way was not to be sniffed

at, especially when the work in question could be highly lucrative and extensive.

'And if you're concerned about your pay,' he continued, 'Rest assured that you will be earning exactly the same rate as you were for the job you just so successfully completed.'

'I'm not concerned about the money!'

'Why don't you want to come? It'll be a holiday.'

'You don't need me there, not really.'

'You have no idea what I need or don't need,' Alessio murmured softly.

'You might change your mind when you see what else I have to show you.' But already she was trying to staunch the wave of anticipation at the thought of going abroad with him, having a few more days in his company, feeding her silly addiction.

She rescued papers from the bottom of the folder, pushed them across to him and watched carefully as he rifled through them.

But then, the moment felt too private, and she stood up and began getting them both a couple of cups of coffee.

What would he be thinking? she wondered as he looked at the little collection of articles about him which she had found in a scrap book in Rachel's room. Again, no attempt had been made to conceal them. Rachel had collected bits and pieces about her father over the years; there were photographs as well, which she must have taken from an album somewhere. Photos of him as a young man.

Eventually, when she could no longer pretend to be taking her time with the coffee, she handed a mug to him and sat back down.

'You found these...' Alessio cleared his throat but he couldn't look her in the eyes.

'I found them,' Lesley said gently. 'So, you see, your daughter isn't quite as indifferent to you as you might believe. Having the conversation you need to have with her might not be quite so difficult as you imagine.'

CHAPTER SIX

'THIS IS QUITE a surprise.' This was all Alessio could find to say and he knew that it was inadequate. His daughter had been collecting a scrap book about him. That reached deep down to a part of him he'd thought no longer existed. He stared down at the most recent cutting of him printed off the Internet. He had had an article written in the business section of the *Financial Times* following the acquisition of a small, independent bank in Spain. It was a poor picture but she had still printed it off and shoved it inside the scrap book.

What was he to think?

He rested his forehead against his clenched fist and drew in a long breath.

A wave of compassion washed over Lesley. Alessio Baldini was tough, cool, controlled. If he hadn't already told her, his entire manner was indicative of someone who knew that they could get what he wanted simply by snapping his fingers. It was a trait she couldn't abide in anyone.

She hated rich men who acted as though they owned the world and everything in it.

She hated men who felt that they could fling money at any problem and, lo and behold, a solution would be forthcoming.

And she hated anyone who didn't value the importance of family life. Family was what grounded you, made you put everything into perspective; stopped you from ever taking yourself too seriously or sacrificing too much in pursuit of your goals.

Alessio acted as he if he owned the world and he certainly acted as though money was the root of solving all problems. If he was a victim of circumstances when it came to an unfortunate family life, then he definitely did not behave as though now was the time when he could begin sorting it out.

So why was she now reaching out to place her hand on his arm? Why had she pulled her chair just that little bit nearer to his so that she could feel the heat radiating from his body?

Was it because the vulnerability she had always sensed in him whenever the subject of his daughter came up was now so glaringly obvious?

Rachel was his Achilles heel; in a flash of comprehension, Lesley saw that. In every other area, Alessio was in complete control of his surroundings, of his *life*, but when it came to his daughter he floundered.

The women he had dated in the past had been kept at a distance. Once bitten, twice shy, and after his experiences with Bianca he had made sure never to let any other woman get past the steel walls that surrounded him. They would never have glimpsed the man who was at a loss when it came to his daughter. She wondered how many of them even *knew* that he had a daughter.

But here she was. She had seen him at his most naked, emotionally.

That was a good thing, she thought, and a bad thing. It was good insofar as everyone needed a sounding board when it came to dark thoughts and emotions.

Those were burdens that could not be carried single-handed. He might have passed the years with his deepest thoughts locked away, but there was no way he would ever have been able to eradicate them, and letting them out could only be a good thing.

With this situation, he had been forced to reveal more about those thoughts to her than he ever had to anyone else. She was certain of that.

The down side was that, for a proud man, the necessity of having to confide thoughts normally hidden would eventually be seen as a sign of weakness.

The sympathetic, listening ear would only work for so long before it turned into a source of resentment.

But did that matter? Really? They wouldn't be around one another for much longer and right here, right now, in some weird, unspoken way, he needed her. She *felt* it, even though it was something he would never, ever articulate.

Those cuttings had moved him beyond words. He was trying hard to control his reaction in front of an audience; that was evident in the thickness of the silence.

'You'll have to return that scrap book to where you found it,' he said gruffly when the silence had been stretched to breaking point. 'Leave it with me overnight and I'll give it to you in the morning.'

Lesley nodded. Her hand was still on his arm and he hadn't shrugged it away. She allowed it to travel so that she was stroking upwards, feeling the strength of his muscles straining under the shirt and the definition of his shoulders and collarbone.

Alessio's eyes narrowed on her.

'Are you feeling sorry for me?' His voice was less cold than it should have been. 'Is that a pity caress?'

He had never confided in anyone. He certainly had

never been an object of pity to anyone, any woman, ever. The thought alone was laughable. Women had always hung onto his every word, longed for some small indication that they occupied a more special role in his life than he was willing to admit to them.

Naturally, they hadn't.

Lesley, though…

She was in a different category. The pity caress did not evoke the expected feelings of contempt, impatience and anger that he would have expected.

He caught her hand in his and held on to it.

'It's not a *pity caress.*' Lesley breathed. Her skin burned where he was touching it, a blaze that was stoked by the expression in his eyes: dark, thoughtful, insightful, amused. 'But I know it must be disconcerting, looking through Rachel's scrap book, seeing pictures of yourself there, articles cut out or printed off from the Internet.' He still wasn't saying anything. He was still just staring at her, his head slightly to one side, his expression brooding and intent.

Her voice petered out and she stared right back at him, eyes wide. She could barely breathe. The moment seemed as fragile as a droplet of water balancing on the tip of a leaf, ready to fall and splinter apart.

She didn't want the moment to end. It was wrong, she knew that, but still she wanted to touch his face and smooth away those very human, very uncertain feelings she knew he would be having; feelings he would be taking great care of to conceal.

'The scrap book was just lying there,' she babbled away as she continued to get lost in his eyes. 'On the bed. I would have felt awful if I had found it hidden under the mattress or at the bottom of a drawer somewhere, but it was just there, waiting to be found.'

'Not by me. Rachel knew that I would never go into her suite of rooms.'

Lesley shrugged. 'I wanted you to see that you're important to your daughter,' she murmured shakily, 'Even if you don't think you are because of the way she acts. Teenagers can be very awkward when it comes to showing their feelings.' He still wasn't saying anything. If he thought that she felt sorry for him, then how was it that he was staying put, not angrily stalking off? 'You remember being a teenager.' She tried a smile in an attempt to lighten the screaming tension between them.

'Vaguely. When I think back to my teenage years, I inevitably end up thinking back to being a daddy before I was out of them.'

'Of course,' Lesley murmured, her voice warm with understanding. At the age of fourteen, not even knowing it, he would have been a mere four years away from becoming a father. It was incredible.

'You're doing it again,' Alessio said under his breath.

'Doing what?'

'Smothering me with your sympathy. Don't worry. Maybe I like it.' His mouth curved into a wolfish smile but underneath that, he thought with passing confusion, her sympathy was actually very welcome.

He reached out and touched her face, then ran two fingers along her cheek, circling her mouth then along her slender neck, coming to rest at the base of her collarbone.

'Have you felt what I've been feeling for the past couple of days?' he asked.

Lesley wasn't sure she was physically capable of answering his question. Not with that hand on her collarbone and her brain reliving every inch of its caress as it had touched her cheek and moved sensuously over her mouth.

'Well?' Alessio prompted. He rested his other hand on her thigh and began massaging it, very gently but very thoroughly, just the one spot, but it was enough to make the breath catch in her throat.

'What do you mean? What are you talking about?' As if she didn't know. As if she wasn't constantly aware of the way he unsettled her. And was she conscious that the electricity flowed both ways? Maybe she was. Maybe that was why the situation had seemed so dangerous.

She had thought that she needed to get out because her attraction to him was getting too much, was threatening to become evident. Maybe a part of her had known that the real reason she needed to get out was because, on some level, she knew that he was attracted to her as well. That underneath the light-hearted flirting there was a very real undercurrent of mutual sexual chemistry.

And that was not good, not at all. She didn't do one-night stands, or two-day stands, or 'going nowhere so why not have a quick romp?' stands.

She did *relationships*. If there had been no guy in her life for literally years, then it was because she had never been the kind of girl who had sex just for the sake of it.

But with Alessio something told her that she could be that girl, and that scared her.

'You know exactly what I mean. You want me. I want you. I've wanted you for a while…'

'I should go up to bed.' Lesley breathed unevenly, nailed to the spot and not moving an inch despite her protestations. 'Leave you to your thoughts…'

'Maybe I'm not that keen on being alone with my thoughts,' Alessio said truthfully. 'Maybe my thoughts are a black hole into which I have no desire to fall.

Maybe I want your pity and your sympathy because they can save me from that fall.'

And what happens when you've been saved from that fall? What happens to me? You're in a weird place right now and, if I rescue you now, what happens when you leave that weird place and shut the door on it once again?

But those muddled thoughts barely had time to settle before they were blown away by the fiercely exciting thought of being with the man who was leaning towards her, staring at her with such intensity that she wanted to moan.

And, before she could retreat behind more weak protestations, he was cupping the back of her neck and drawing her towards him, very slowly, so slowly that she had time to appreciate the depth of his dark eyes; the fine lines that etched his features; the slow, sexy curve of his mouth; the length of his dark eyelashes.

Lesley fell into the kiss with a soft moan, part resignation, part despair; mostly intense, long-awaited excitement. She spread her hand behind his neck in a mirror gesture to how he was holding her and, as his tongue invaded the soft contours of her mouth, she returned the kiss and let that kiss do its work—spread moisture between her legs, pinch her nipples into tight, sensitive buds, raise the hairs on her arms.

'We shouldn't be doing this,' she muttered, breaking apart for a few seconds and immediately wanting to draw him back towards her again.

'Why not?'

'Because this isn't the right reason for going to bed with someone.'

'Don't know what you're talking about.' He leaned

to kiss her again but she stilled him with a hand on his chest and met his gaze with anxious eyes.

'I don't pity you, Alessio,' she said huskily. 'I'm sorry that you don't have the relationship with your daughter that you'd like, but I don't pity you. And when I showed you that scrap book it was because I felt the contents were something you needed to know about. What I feel is…understanding and compassion.'

'And what I feel is that we shouldn't get lost in words.'

'Because words are not your thing?' But she smiled and felt a rush of tenderness towards this strong, powerful man who was also capable of being so wonderfully *human*, hard though he might try to fight it.

'You know what they say about actions speaking louder…' He grinned at her. His body was on fire. She was right—words weren't his thing, at least not the words that made up long, involved conversations about feelings. He scooped her up and she gave a little cry of surprise, then wriggled and told him to put her down immediately; she might be slim but she was way too tall for him to start thinking he could play the caveman with her.

Alessio ignored her and carried her up the stairs to his bedroom.

'Every woman likes a caveman.' He gently kicked open his bedroom door and then deposited her on his king-sized bed.

Night had crept up without either of them realising it and, without the bedroom lights switched on, the darkness only allowed them to see one another in shadowy definition.

'I don't,' Lesley told him breathlessly as he stood in front of her and began unbuttoning his shirt.

She had already seen him barely clothed in the pool. She should know what to expect when it came to his body and yet, as he tossed his shirt carelessly on the ground, it was as if she was looking at him for the first time.

The impact he had on her was as new, as raw, as powerful.

But then, this was different, wasn't it? This wasn't a case of watching him covertly from the sidelines as he covered a few lengths in a swimming pool.

This was lying on his bed, in a darkened room, with the promise of possession flicking through her like a spreading fire.

Alessio didn't want to talk. He wanted to take her, fast and hard, until he heard her cry out with satisfaction. He wanted to pleasure her and feel her come with him inside her.

But how much sweeter to take his time, to taste every inch of her, to withstand the demands of his raging hormones and indulge in making love with her at a more leisurely pace.

'No?' he drawled, hand resting on the zipper of his trousers before he began taking those off as well, where they joined the shirt in a heap on the ground, leaving him in just his boxers. 'You think I'm a caveman because I carried you up the stairs?'

He slowly removed his boxers. He regretted not having turned some lights on because he would have liked to really appreciate the expression on her face as he watched her watching him. He strolled towards the side of the bed and stood there, then he touched himself lightly and heard her swift intake of breath.

'I just think you're a caveman in general,' Lesley feasted her eyes on his impressive erection. When he held it in his hand, she longed to do the same to herself, to touch herself down there. Her nerves were stretched to breaking point and she wished she was just a little more experienced, a little more knowing about what to do when it came to a man like him, a man who probably knew everything there was to know about the opposite sex.

She sat up, crossed her legs and reached out to touch him, replacing his hand with hers and gaining confidence as she felt him shudder with appreciation.

It was a strange turn-on to be fully clothed while he was completely naked.

'Is that right?'

As she took him into her mouth, Alessio grunted and flung his head back. He had died and gone to heaven. The wetness of her mouth on his hard erection, the way she licked, teased and tasted, his fingers curled into her short hair, made him breathe heavily, well aware that he had to come down from this peak or risk bringing this love-making session to an extremely premature conclusion, which was not something he intended to do.

With a sigh of pure regret, he eased her off him.

Then he joined her on the bed. 'Would I be a caveman if I stripped you? I wouldn't…' he slipped his fingers underneath the tee-shirt and began easing it over her head '…want to…' Then came the jeans, which she wriggled out of so that she remained in bra and pants, white, functional items of clothing that looked wonderfully wholesome on her. 'Offend your feminist sensibilities.'

For the life of her, Lesley couldn't find where she had misplaced those feminist sensibilities which he had mentioned. She reached behind to unhook her bra but he gently drew her hands away so that he could accomplish the task himself.

He half-closed his eyes and his nostrils flared with rampant appreciation of her small but perfectly formed breasts. Her nipples were big, brown, circular discs. She had propped herself up on both elbows and her breasts were small, pointed mounds offering themselves to him like sweet, delicate fruit.

In one easy movement, he straddled her, and she fell back against the pillow with a soft, excited moan.

She was wet for him. As he reached behind him to slip his hand under the panties, she groaned and covered her eyes with one hand.

'I want to see you, my darling.' Alessio lowered himself so that he was lightly on top of her. 'Move your hand.'

'I don't usually do this sort of thing,' Lesley mumbled. 'I'm not into one-night stands. I never have been. I don't see the point.'

'Shh.' He gazed down at her until she was burning all over. Then he gently began licking her breast, moving in a concentric circle until his tongue found her nipple. The sensitised tip had peaked into an erect nub, and as he took her whole nipple into his mouth so that he could suckle on it she quivered under him, moving with feverish urgency, arching back so that not a single atom of the pleasurable sensations zinging through her was lost.

She had to get rid of her panties, they were damp and uncomfortable, but with his big body over hers she couldn't reach them. Instead she clasped her hand to the back of his head and pressed him down harder on her breasts, giving little cries and whimpers as he carried on sucking and teasing, moving between her breasts and then, when she was going crazy from it, he trailed his tongue over her rib cage and down to the indentation of her belly button.

His breath on her body was warm and she was breathing fast, hardly believing that what was happening really was happening and yet desperate for it to continue, desperate to carry on shamelessly losing herself in the moment.

He felt her sharp intake of breath as he slipped her underwear down, and then she was holding her breath as he gently parted her legs and flicked his tongue over her core.

Lesley groaned. This was an intimacy she had not experienced before. She curled her fingers into his dark hair and tugged him but her body was responding with a shocking lack of inhibition as he continued to taste her, teasing her swollen bud until she lost the ability to think clearly.

Alessio felt her every response as if their bodies had tuned into the same wavelength. In a blinding, revelatory flash, he realised that everything else that had come before with women could not compete with what was happening right now, because this woman had just seen far more of him than anyone else ever had.

This had not been a simple game of pursuit and capture. She hadn't courted this situation, nor had he anticipated it. Certainly, there had come a point when he had looked at her and liked what he had seen; had wanted what he had seen; had even vaguely *planned* on having her because, when it came to him and women, wanting and having were always the same side of the coin.

But he knew that he hadn't banked on what was happening between them now. For the first time, he had the strangest feeling that this wasn't just about sex.

But the sex was great.

He swept aside all his unravelling thoughts and lost himself in her body, in her sweet little whimpers and her broken groans as she wriggled under him, until at last, when he could feel her wanting to reach her orgasm, he broke off to fumble in the bedside cabinet for a condom.

Lesley could hardly bear that brief pause. She was alive in a way she had never been before and that terrified her. Her relationships with the opposite sex had always been guarded and imbued with a certain amount of defensiveness that stemmed from her own private insecurities.

Having been raised in an all-male family, she had developed brilliant coping skills when it came to standing her ground with the opposite sex. Her brothers had toughened her up and taught her the value of healthy competition, the benefits of never being cowed by a guy, of knowing that she could hold her own.

But no one had been able to help her during those teenage years when the lines of distinction between boys and girls were drawn. She had watched from the sidelines and decided that lipstick and mascara were not for her, that sport was far more enjoyable. It wasn't about how you looked, it was about what was inside you and what was inside her—her intelligence, her sense of humour, her capacity for compassion—did not need to be camouflaged with make-up and sexy clothes.

The only guys she had ever been attracted to were the ones who'd seen her for the person she was, the ones whose heads hadn't swivelled round when a busty blonde in a short skirt had walked past.

So what, it flashed through her head, was she doing with Alessio Baldini?

She sighed and reached up to him as he settled back on her, nudging her legs apart, then she closed her eyes and was transported to another planet as he thrust into her, deep and hard, building a rhythm that drove everything out of her mind.

She flung her head back and succumbed to loud, responsive cries as he continued to fill her.

She came on a tidal wave of intense pleasure and felt her whole body shudder and arch up towards him in a wonderful fusing of bodies.

The moment seemed to last for ever and she was only brought back down to earth when he withdrew from her and cursed fluently under his breath.

'The condom has split.'

Lesley abruptly surfaced from the pleasant, dreamy cloud on which she had been happily drifting, and the uncomfortable thoughts which had been sidelined when he had begun touching her returned with double intensity.

What on earth had she done? How could she have allowed herself to end up in bed with this man? Had she lost her mind? This was a situation that was going nowhere and would never go anywhere. She was Lesley Fox, a practical, clever, not at all sexy woman who should have known better than to be sweet talked into sleeping with a man who wouldn't have looked twice at her under normal circumstances.

On every level, he was just the sort of man she usually wouldn't have gone near and, had he seen her passing on the street, she certainly would not have been the sort of woman he would have noticed. She would literally have been invisible to him because she just wasn't his type.

Fate had thrown them together and an attraction had built between them but she knew that she would be a complete fool not to recognise that that attraction was grounded in novelty.

'How the hell could that have happened?' Alessio said, his voice dark with barely contained anger. 'This is the last thing I need right now.'

Lesley got that. He had found himself tricked into marriage by a pregnancy he had not courted once upon a time and his entire adult life had been affected. Of course he would not want to repeat that situation.

Yet, she couldn't help but feel the sting of hurt at the simmering anger in his voice.

'It won't happen,' she said stiffly. She wriggled into a sitting position and watched as he vaulted upright and began searching around for his boxers, having disposed of the faulty condom.

'And you know that because?'

'It's the wrong time of month for that to happen.' She surreptitiously crossed her fingers and tried to calculate when she had last had her period. 'And, rest assured, the last thing I would want would be to end up pregnant, Alessio. As it stands, this was a very bad idea.'

In the process of locating a tee-shirt from a chest of drawers, he paused and strolled back to the bed. The condom had split and there was nothing he could do about that now. He could only hope that she was right, that they were safe.

But, that aside, how could she say that making love had been a very bad idea? He was oddly affronted.

'You know what. This. Us. Ending up in bed together. It shouldn't have happened.'

'Why not? We're attracted to one another. How could it have been a bad idea? I was under the impression that you had actually enjoyed the experience.' He looked down at her and felt his libido begin to rise once again.

'That's not the point.' She swung her legs over the side of the bed and stood up, conscious of her nudity, gritting her teeth against the temptation to drag the covers off the bed and shield herself from him.

'God, you're beautiful.'

Lesley flushed and looked away, stubbornly proud, and refusing to believe that he meant a word of that. Novelty was a beautiful thing but became boring very quickly.

'Well?' He caught her wrist and tilted her face so that she had no option but to look at him.

'Well what?' Lesley muttered, lowering her eyes.

'Well, let's go back to bed.'

'Didn't you hear a word I just said?'

'Every word.' He kissed her delicately on the corner of her mouth and then very gently on her lips.

In a heartbeat, and to her disgust, Lesley could feel her determination begin to melt away.

'You're not my type,' she mumbled, refusing to cave in, but his lips were so soft against her jaw that her disobedient body was responding in all sorts of stupidly predictable ways.

'Because I'm a caveman?'

'Yes!' Her hands crept up to his neck and she protested feebly as he lifted her off her feet and back towards the bed to which she had only minutes previously sworn not to return.

'So, what are you looking for in a man?' Alessio murmured.

This time, he drew the covers over them. It was very dark outside. Even with the curtains open, the night was black velvet with only a slither of moon penetrating the darkness and weakly illuminating the bedroom.

He could feel her reluctance, her mind fighting her body, and it felt imperative that her body win the battle because he wanted her, more than he had ever wanted any woman in his life before.

'Not someone like you, Alessio,' Lesley whispered, pressing her hands flat against his chest and feeling the steady beat of his heart.

'Why? Why not someone like me?'

'Because...' *Because safety was not with a man who looked like him, a man who could have anyone he wanted.* She knew her limits. She knew that she was just not the sort of girl who drew guys to her like a magnet. She never had been. She just didn't have the confidence; had never had the right preparation; had never had a mother's guiding hand to show her the way to all those little feminine wiles that went into the mix of attraction between the sexes.

But bigger than her fear of involvement with him was her fear of *not* getting involved, *not* taking the chance.

'You're just not the sort of person I ever imagined having any kind of relationship with, that's all.'

'We're not talking marriage here, Lesley, we're talking about enjoying each other.' He propped himself up on one elbow and traced his finger along her arm. 'I'm not looking for commitment any more than you probably are.'

And certainly not with someone like you; Lesley reluctantly filled in the remainder of that remark.

'And you still haven't told me the sort of man you would call "your type".' She was warm and yielding in his arms. She might make a lot of noises about this being a mistake, but she wanted him as much as he wanted her, and he knew that if he slipped his fingers into her he would feel the tell-tale proof of her arousal.

He could have her right here and right now, despite whatever she said about him not being her type. And who, in the end, cared whether he was her type or not? Hadn't he just told her that this wasn't about commitment and marriage? In other words, did it really matter if he wasn't her type?

But he was piqued at the remark. She was forthright and spoke her mind; he had become accustomed to that very quickly. But surely what she had said amounted to an unacceptable lack of tact! He thought that there was nothing wrong in asking her to explain exactly what she had meant.

His voice had dropped a few shades.

'You're offended, aren't you?' Lesley asked and Alessio was quick to deny any such thing.

Lesley could have kicked herself for asking him that question. Of course he wouldn't be offended! To be offended, he would actually have had to care about her and that was not the case here, as he had made patently clear.

'That's a relief!' she exclaimed lightly. 'My type? I guess thoughtful, caring, sensitive; someone who believes in the same things that I do, who has similar interests…maybe even someone working in the same field. You know—artistic, creative, not really bothered about the whole business of making money.'

Alessio bared his teeth in a smile. 'Sounds a lot of fun. Sure someone like that would be able to keep up with you? No, scrap that—too much talk. There are better things to do and, now that we've established that you can't resist me even though I'm the last kind of person you would want in your life, let's make love.'

'Alessio…'

He stifled any further protest with a long, lingering kiss that released in her a sigh of pure resignation. So this made no sense, so she was a complete idiot…

Where had the practical, level-headed girl with no illusions about herself gone? All she seemed capable of doing was giving in.

'And,' he murmured into her ear. 'In case you think that Italy is off the agenda because I'm not a touchy-feely art director for a design company, forget it. I still want you there by my side. Trust me, I will make it worth your while.'

CHAPTER SEVEN

EVERYTHING SEEMED TO happen at the speed of light after that. Of course, there was no inconvenient hanging around for affordable flights or having to surf the Internet for places to stay. None of the usual headaches dogged Alessio's spur-of-the-moment decision to take Lesley to Italy.

Two days after he had extended his invitation, they were boarding a plane to Italy.

It was going to be a surprise visit. Armed with information, they were going to get the full story from his daughter, lay all the cards on the table and then, when they were back in the UK, Alessio would sort the other half of the equation out. He would pay an informal visit to his emailing friend and he was sure that they would reach a happy conclusion where no money changed hands.

Lessons, he had assured her, would regrettably have to be learnt.

Lesley privately wondered what his approach to his daughter would be. Would similar lessons also 'regrettably have to be learnt'? How harsh would those lessons be? He barely had a relationship with Rachel and she privately wondered how he intended ever to build on it if he went in to 'sort things out' with the diplomacy of a bull in a china shop.

That was one of the reasons she had agreed to go to Italy with him.

Without saying it in so many words, she knew that he was looking to her for some sort of invisible moral back-up, even though he had stated quite clearly that he needed her there primarily to impart the technicalities of what she had discovered should the situation demand it.

'You haven't said anything for the past half an hour.' Alessio interrupted her train of thought as they were shown into the first class cabin of the plane. 'Why?'

Lesley bristled. 'I was just thinking how fast everything's moved,' she said as they were shown to seats as big as armchairs and invited to have a glass of champagne, which she refused.

She stole a glance at his sexy face, lazy and amused at the little show of rebellion.

'I came to do a job for you, thinking that I would be in and out of your house in a matter of a few hours and now here I am, days later, boarding a plane for Italy.'

'I know. Isn't life full of adventure and surprise?' He waved aside an awe-struck air hostess and settled into the seat next to her. 'I confess that I myself am surprised at the way things unfolded. Surprised but not displeased.'

'Because you've got what you wanted,' Lesley complained. She was so accustomed to her independence that she couldn't help feeling disgruntled at the way she had been railroaded into doing exactly what he had wanted her to do.

Even though, a little voice inside her pointed out, this rollercoaster ride was the most exciting thing she had ever done in her life—even though it was scary, even though it had yanked her out of her precious comfort zone, even though she knew that it would come to nothing and the fall back to Planet Earth would be painful.

'I didn't force your hand,' Alessio said comfortably.

'You went into the office and talked to my boss.'

'I just wanted to point out the world of opportunity lying at his feet if he could see his way to releasing you for one week to accompany me to Italy.'

'I dread to think what the office grapevine is going to make of this situation.'

'Do you care what anyone thinks?' He leant against the window so that he could direct one hundred per cent of his undivided attention on her.

'Of course I do!' Lesley blushed because she knew that, whilst she might give the impression of being strong, sassy and outspoken, she still had a basic need to be liked and accepted. She just wasn't always good at showing that side of herself. In fact, she was uncomfortably aware of the fact that, whilst Alessio might have shown her more of himself than he might have liked, she had likewise done the same.

He would not know it, but against all odds she had allowed herself to walk into unchartered territory, to have a completely new experience with a man knowing that he was not the right man for her.

'Relax and enjoy the ride,' he murmured.

'I'm not going to enjoy confronting your daughter with all the information we've managed to uncover. She's going to know that I went through her belongings.'

'If Rachel had wanted to keep her private life private, then she should have destroyed all the incriminating evidence. The fact is that she's still a child and she has no vote when it comes to us doing what was necessary to protect her.'

'She may not see it quite like that.'

'She will have to make a very big effort to, in that case.'

Lesley sighed and leaned back into the seat with her eyes shut. What Alessio did with his daughter was really none of her business. Yes, she'd been involved in bringing the situation to light, but its solutions and whatever repercussions followed would be a continuing saga she would leave behind. She would return to the blessed safety of what she knew and the family story of Alessio and his daughter would remain a mystery to her for ever.

So there was no need to feel any compunction about just switching off.

Yet she had to bite back the temptation to tell him what she thought, even though she knew that he would have every right to dismiss whatever advice she had to offer about the peculiarity of their relationship, if a 'relationship' was what it could be called. She was his lover, a woman who probably knew far too much about his life for his liking. She had been paid to investigate a personal problem, yet had no right to have any discussions about that problem, even though they were sleeping together.

In a normal relationship, she should have felt free to speak her mind, but this was not a normal relationship, was it? For either of them. She had sacrificed her feminist principles for sex and she still couldn't understand herself, nor could she understand how it was that she felt no regrets.

In fact, when he looked at her the way he was looking at her right now, all she felt was a dizzying need to have him take her.

If only he could see into her mind and unravel all her doubts and uncertainties. Thank goodness he couldn't. As far as he was concerned, she was a tough career woman with as little desire for a long-term relationship as him. They had both stepped out of the box, drawn to each other by a combination of proximity and the pull of novelty.

'You're thinking,' Alessio said drily. 'Why don't you spit it out and then we can get it out of the way?'

'Get what out of the way?'

'Whatever disagreements you have about the way I intend to handle this situation.'

'You hate it when I tell you what I think,' Lesley said with asperity. Alessio shrugged and continued looking at her in the way that made her toes curl and her mouth run dry.

'And I don't like it when I can see you thinking but you're saying nothing. "Between a rock and a hard place" comes to mind.' He was amazed at how easily he had adapted to her outspoken approach. His immediate instinct now was not to shove her back behind his boundary lines and remind her about overstepping the mark.

'I just don't think you should confront Rachel and demand to know what the hell is going on.' She shifted in the big seat and turned so that she was completely facing him.

The plane was beginning to taxi in preparation for taking off, and she fell silent for a short while as the usual canned talk was given about safety exits, but as soon as they were airborne she looked at him worriedly once again.

'It's hard to know how to get answers if you don't ask for them,' he pointed out.

'We know the situation.'

'And I want to know how it got to where it finally got. It's one thing knowing the outcome but I don't intend to let history repeat itself.'

'You might want to try a little sympathy.'

Alessio snorted.

'You said yourself that she's just a kid,' Lesley reminded him gently.

'You *could* always spare me the horror of making a mess of things by talking to Rachel yourself,' he said.

'She's not my daughter.'

'Then allow me to work this one out myself.' But he knew that she was right. There was no tactful way of asking the questions he would have to ask, and if his daughter disliked him now then she was about to dislike him a whole lot more when he was finished talking to her.

Of course, there were those photos, cuttings of him—some indication, as Lesley had said, that she wasn't completely indifferent to the fact that he was her father.

But would that be enough to take them past this little crisis? Unlikely. Especially when she discovered that the photos and cuttings had been salvaged in an undercover operation.

'Okay.'

Alessio had looked away, out through the window to the dense bank of cloud over which they were flying. Now, he turned to Lesley with a frown.

'Okay. I'll talk to Rachel if you like,' she said on a reluctant sigh.

'Why would you do that?'

Why would she? Because she couldn't bear to see him looking the way he was looking now, with the hopeless expression of someone staring defeat in the face.

And why did she care? she asked herself. But she shied away from trying to find an answer to that.

'Because I'm on the outside of this mess. If she directs all her teenage anger at me, then by the time she gets to you some of it may have diffused.'

'And the likelihood of that is…?' But he was touched at her generosity of spirit.

'Not good odds,' Lesley conceded. 'But worth a try, don't you think?' He was staring at her with an expression of intense curiosity and she continued quickly, before he could interrupt with the most obvious question: *why?* A question to which she had no answer. 'Besides, I'm good at mediating. I got a lot of practice at doing that when I was growing up. When there are six kids in a family, a dad worked off his feet, and five of those six are boys, there's always lots of opportunity to practise mediation skills.'

But just no opportunity to practise *being a girl*. And that was why she was the way she was now: hesitant in relationships; self-conscious about whether she had what it took to make any relationship last; willing not to get into the water at all rather than diving in and finding herself out of her depth and unable to cope.

Only since Alessio had appeared on the scene had she really seen the pattern in her behaviour, the way she kept guys, smiling, at arm's length.

He was so dramatically different from any man she had ever been remotely drawn to that it had been easy to pinpoint her own lack of self-confidence. She was a clever career woman with a bright life ahead of her and yet that sinfully beautiful face had reduced all those achievements to rubble.

She had looked at him and returned to her teenage years when she had simply not known how to approach a boy because she had had no idea what they were looking for.

For her, Alessio Baldini was not the obvious choice

when it came to picking a guy to sleep with, yet sleep with him she had, and she was glad that she had done so. She had broken through the glass barrier that had stood between her and the opposite sex. It was strange, but he had given her confidence she hadn't really even known she had needed.

'And mediation skills are so important when one is growing up,' Alessio murmured.

Basking in her new-found revelations, Lesley smiled. 'No, they're not,' she admitted with more candour than she'd ever done to anyone in her life before. 'In fact, I can't think of any skill a teenage girl has less use for than mediation skills,' she mused. 'But I had plenty of that.' She leaned back and half-closed her eyes. When she next spoke it was almost as though she was talking with no audience listening to what was being said.

'My mum died when I was so young, I barely remember her. I mean, Dad always told us about her, what she was like and such, and there were pictures of her everywhere. But the truth is, I don't have any memories of her—of doing anything with her, if you see what I mean.'

She glanced sideways at him and he nodded. He had always fancied himself as the sort of man who would be completely at sea when it came to listening to women pour their hearts out, hence it was a tendency that he had strenuously discouraged.

Now, though, he was drawn to what she was saying and by the faraway, pensive expression on her face.

'I never thought that I missed having a mother. I never knew what it was like to have one and my dad was always good enough for me. But I can see now that growing up in a male-only family might have given me confidence with the opposite sex but only when it came to things like work and study. I was encouraged to be as good as they were, and I think I succeeded, but I wasn't taught, well…'

'How to wear make-up and shop for dresses?'

'Sounds crazy but I do think girls need to be taught stuff like that.' She looked at him gravely. 'I can see that it's easy to have bags of confidence in one area and not much in another,' she said with a rueful shake of her head. 'When it came to the whole game-playing, sexual attraction thing, I don't think I've ever had loads of confidence.'

'And now?'

'I feel I have, so I guess I should say thank you.'

'*Thank you?* What are you thanking me for?'

'For encouraging me to step out of the box,' Lesley told him with that blend of frankness and disingenuousness which he found so appealing.

Alessio was momentarily distracted from the headache awaiting him in Italy. He had no idea where she was going with this but it had all the feel of a conversation heading down a road he would rather not explore.

'Always happy to oblige,' he said vaguely. 'I hope you've packed light clothes. The heat in Italy is quite different from the heat in England.'

'If I hadn't taken on this job, there's not a chance in the world that I would ever have met you.'

'That's true enough.'

'Not only do we not move in the same circles, we have no interests in common whatsoever.'

Alessio was vaguely indignant at what he thought might be an insult in disguise. Was she comparing him to the 'soul mate' guy she had yet to meet, the touchy-feely one with the artistic side and a love of all things natural?

'And if we *had* ever met, at a social do or something like that, I would never have had the confidence to approach you.'

'I'm not sure where you're going with this.'

'Here's what I'm saying, Alessio. I feel as though I've taken huge strides in gaining self-confidence in certain areas and it's thanks in some measure to you. I could say that I'm going to be a completely different person when I get back to the UK and start dating again.'

Alessio could not believe what he was hearing. He had no idea where this conversation had come from and he was enraged that she could sit there, his lover, and talk about going back on the dating scene!

'The dating scene.'

'Is this conversation becoming a little too deep for you?' Lesley asked with a grin. 'I know you don't do deep when it comes to women and conversations.'

'And how do you know that?'

'Well, you've already told me that you don't like encouraging them to get behind a stove and start cooking a meal for you, just in case they think, I don't know, they have somehow managed to get a foot through the door. So I'm guessing that meaningful conversations are probably on the banned list as well.'

They were. It was true. He had never enjoyed long, emotional conversations which, from experience, always ended up in the same place—invitations to meet the parents, questions about commitment and where the relationship was heading.

In fact, the second that type of conversation began rearing its head, he usually felt a pressing need to end the relationship. He had been coerced into one marriage and he had made a vow never to let himself be railroaded into another similar mistake, however tempting the woman in question might be.

He looked into her astute, brown eyes and scowled. ‘I may not be looking for someone to walk down the aisle with, but that doesn’t mean that I’m not prepared to have meaningful discussions with women. I’m also insulted,’ he was driven to continue, ‘That I’ve been used as some kind of trial run for the real thing.’

‘What do you mean?’ Lesley was feeling good. The vague unease that had been plaguing her ever since she had recognised how affected she was by Alessio had been boxed away with an explanation that made sense.

Sleeping with him had opened her eyes to fears and doubts she had been harbouring for years. She felt that she had buried a lack of self-confidence in her own sexuality under the guise of academic success and then, later on, success in her career. She had dressed in ways that didn’t enhance her own femininity because she had always feared that she lacked what it took.

But then she had slept with him, slept with a man who was way out of her league, had been wanted and desired by him, and made to feel proud of the way she looked.

Was it any wonder that he had such a dramatic effect on her? It was a case of lust mixed up with a hundred other things.

But the bottom line was that he was no more than a learning curve for her. When she thought about it like that, it made perfect sense. It also released her from the disturbing suspicion that she was way too deep in a non-relationship that was going nowhere, a relationship that meant far more to her than it did to him.

Learning curves provided lessons and, once those lessons had been learnt, it was always easy to move on.

Learning curves didn't result in broken hearts.

She breathed in quickly and shakily. 'Well?' she flung at him, while her mind continued to chew over the notion that her involvement with him had been fast and hard. She had been catapulted into a world far removed from hers, thrown into the company of a man who was very, very different from the sort of men she was used to, and certainly worlds apart from the sort of man she would ever have expected herself to be attracted to.

But common sense had been no match for the power of his appeal and now here she was.

When she thought about never seeing him again, she felt faintly, sickeningly panicked.

What did that mean? Her thoughts became muddled when she tried to work her way through what suddenly seemed a dangerous, uncertain quagmire.

'I mean that you used me,' Alessio said bluntly. 'I don't like being used. And I don't appreciate you talking about jumping back into the dating scene, not when we're still lovers. I expect the women I sleep with to only have eyes for me.'

The unbridled arrogance of that statement, which was so fundamentally *Alessio,* brought a reluctant smile to her lips.

She had meant it when she had told him that under normal circumstances they would never have met. Their paths simply wouldn't have crossed. He didn't mix in the same circles as she did. And, even if by some freak chance they *had* met, they would have looked at one another and quickly looked away.

She would have seen a cold, wealthy, arrogant cardboard cut-out and he would have seen, well, a woman who was nothing like the sort of women he went out with and therefore she'd have been invisible. But the circumstances that had brought them together had uniquely provided them with a different insight into one another.

She had seen beneath the veneer to the three-dimensional man and he had seen through the sassy, liberal-minded, outspoken woman in charge of her life to the uncertain, insecure girl.

She was smart enough to realise, however, that that changed nothing. He was and always would be uninterested in any relationship that demanded longevity. He was shaped by his past and his main focus now was his daughter and trying to resolve the difficult situation that had arisen there. He might have slept with her because she was so different from what he was used to and because she was there, ready and willing but, whereas he had fundamentally reached deep and changed her, she hadn't done likewise with him.

'You're smiling.' Alessio was reluctant to abandon the conversation. When, he thought, was this dive back into the dating scene going to begin? Had she put time limits on what they had? Wasn't he usually the one to do that?

'I don't want to argue with you.' Lesley kept that smile pinned to her face. 'Who will you introduce me as when we get to Italy?'

'I haven't given it any thought. Where is all this hectic dating going to take place?'

'I beg your pardon?'

'You can't start conversations you don't intend to finish. So, where will you be going to meet Mr Right? I'm taking it you intend to start hunting when we return to England, or will you be looking around Italy for any suitable candidates?'

'Are you upset because I said what I said?'

'Why would I be upset?'

'I have no idea,' Lesley said as flippantly as she could. 'Because we both know that what we have isn't going to last.' She allowed just a fraction of a second in which he could have contradicted her, but of course he said nothing, and that hurt and reinforced for her the position she held in his life. 'And of course I'm not going to be looking around Italy for suitable candidates. I haven't forgotten why I'll be there in the first place.'

'Good,' Alessio said brusquely.

But the atmosphere between them had changed, and when he flipped open his lap-top and began working Lesley took the hint and excavated her own lap-top so that she too could begin working, even though she couldn't concentrate.

What she had said had put his nose out of joint, she decided. He wanted her to be his, to belong to him for however long he deemed it suitable, until the time came when he got bored of her and decided that it was time for her to go. For her to talk to him about dating other men would have been a blow to his masculine pride, hence his reaction. He wasn't upset, nor was he jealous of these imaginary men she would soon be seeking out. If they existed.

Her thoughts drifted and meandered until the plane began its descent. Then they were touching down at the airport in Liguria and everything vanished, except the reason why they were here in the first place.

Even the bright sunshine vanished as they stepped out and were ushered into a chauffeur-driven car to begin the journey to his house on the peninsula.

'I used to come here far more frequently in the past,'

he mused as he tried to work out the last time he had visited his coastal retreat.

'And then what happened?' It was her first time in Italy and she had to drag her eyes away from the lush green of the backdrop, the mountains that reared up to one side, the flora which was eye-wateringly exuberant.

'Life seemed to take over.' He shrugged. 'I woke up to the fact that Bianca had as little to do with this part of Italy as she possibly could and, of course, where she went, my daughter was dragged along. My interest died over a period of time and, anyway, work prohibited the sort of lengthy holidays that do this place justice.'

'Why didn't you just sell up?'

'I had no pressing reason to. Now I'm glad I hung onto the place. It may have been a bit uncomfortable had we been under the same roof as Rachel and Claudia, given the circumstances. I hadn't planned on saying anything to my mother-in-law about our arrival, but in all events I decided to spare her the shock of a surprise visit—although I've told her to say nothing to Rachel, for obvious reasons.'

'Those reasons being?'

'I can do without my teenage daughter scarpering.'

'You don't think she would, do you? Where would she go?'

'I should think she knows Italy a lot better than I do. She certainly would have friends in the area I know nothing about. I think it's fair to say that my knowledge of the people she hangs out with isn't exactly comprehensive.' But he smiled and then stared out of the window. 'I shudder to think of Claudia trying to keep control of my daughter on a permanent basis.'

The conversation lapsed. The sun was setting by the time they finally made it to his house, which they approached from the rear and which was perched on a hill top.

The front of the house overlooked a drop down to the sea and the broad wooden-floored veranda, with its deep rattan-framed sofas, was the perfect spot from which you could just sit and watch the changing face of the ocean.

Only when they had settled in, shown to their bedroom by a housekeeper—yet another employee keeping a vacant house going—did Alessio inform her that he intended visiting his mother-in-law later that evening.

'It won't be too late for her,' he said, prowling through the bedroom and then finally moving to the window to stare outside. He turned to look at her. In loose-fitting trousers and a small, silky vest, she looked spectacular. It unsettled him to think that, even with this pressing business to conclude, she had still managed to distract him to the point where all he could think of was her returning to London and joining the singles scene.

He wouldn't have said that his ego was so immense that it could be so easily bruised, but his teeth clamped together in grim rejection of the thought of any man touching her. Since when had he been the possessive type, let alone jealous?

'It will also allow Rachel to sleep on everything, give her time to put things into perspective and to come to terms with returning with us on the next flight over.'

'You make it sound as though we'll be leaving tomorrow.' Lesley hovered by the bed, sensing his mood and wondering whether it stemmed from parental concern at what was to come. She wanted to reach out and comfort him but knew, with unerring instinct, that that would be the last thing he wanted.

Yet hadn't he implied that they would be in the country for at least a week? She wondered why the rush was suddenly on to get out as quickly as possible. Did he really think that she had been using him? Had he decided that the sooner he was rid of her, the better, now that she had bucked the trend of all his other women and displayed a lack of suitable clinginess?

Pride stopped her from asking for any inconvenient explanations.

'Not that it matters when we leave,' she hastened to add. 'Would I have time to have a shower?'

'Of course. I have some work I need to get through anyway. I can use the time to do that and you can meet me downstairs in the sitting room. Unlike my country estate, you should be able to find your way around this villa without the use of a map.'

He smiled, and Lesley smiled back and muttered something suitable, but she was dismayed to feel a lump gathering at the back of her throat.

The sex between them was so hot that she would have expected him to have given her that wolfish grin of his, to have joined her in the shower, to have forgotten what they had come here for...just for a while.

Instead, he was vanishing through the door without a backward glance and she had to swallow back her bitter disappointment.

Once showered, and in a pair of faded jeans and a loose tee-shirt, she found him waiting for her in the sitting room, pacing while he jangled car keys in his pocket. The chauffeur had departed in the saloon car in which they had been ferried and she wondered how they were going to get to Claudia's villa, but there was a small four-wheel-drive jeep tucked away at the side of the house.

She had all the paperwork in a backpack which she

had slung over her shoulder. 'I hope I'm not underdressed,' she said suddenly, looking up at him. 'I don't know how formal your mother-in-law is.'

'You're fine,' Alessio reassured her. A sudden image of her naked body flashed through his head with such sudden force that his heart seemed to skip a beat. He should have his mind one hundred per cent focused on the situation about to unravel, he told himself impatiently, instead of thinking about her and whatever life choices she decided to make. 'Your dress code isn't the issue here,' he said abruptly and Lesley nodded and turned away.

'I know that,' she returned coolly. 'I just wouldn't want to offend anyone.'

Alessio thought that that was rather shutting the door after the horse had bolted, considering she had had no trouble in offending *him*, but it was such a ridiculous thought that he swept it aside and offered a conciliatory smile.

'Don't think that I don't appreciate what you're doing,' he told her in a low voice. 'You didn't have to come here.'

'Even though you made sure I did by dangling that carrot of a fabulous new big job under my boss's nose?' She was still edgy at his dismissive attitude towards her but, when he looked at her like that, his dark eyes roving over her face, her body did its usual thing and leapt into heated response.

As if smelling that reaction, Alessio felt some of the tension leave his body and this time when he smiled it was with genuine, sexy warmth.

'I've always liked using all the tools in my box,' he murmured and Lesley shot him a fledgling grin.

His black mood had evaporated. She could sense it.

Perhaps now that they were about to leave some of his anxiety about what lay ahead was filtering away, replaced by a sense of the inevitable.

At any rate, she just wanted to enjoy this return to normality between them. For that little window when there had been tension between them, she had felt awful. She knew that she had to get a grip, had to put this little escapade into perspective.

She would give herself the remainder of what time was left in Italy and then, once they returned to the UK, whatever the outcome of what happened here, she would return to the life she had temporarily left behind. She had already laid the groundwork for a plausible excuse, one that would allow her to retreat with her dignity and pride intact.

It was time to leave this family saga behind her.

CHAPTER EIGHT

THE DRIVE TO Claudia's villa took under half an hour. He told her that he hadn't been back to Portofino for a year and a half, and then it had been a flying visit, but he still seemed to remember the narrow roads effortlessly.

They arrived at a house that was twice the size of Alessio's. 'Bianca always had a flair for the flamboyant,' he said drily as he killed the engine and they both stared at an imposing villa fronted by four Romanesque columns, the middle two standing on either side of a bank of shallow steps that led to the front door. 'When we were married and she discovered that money was no object, she made it her mission to spend. As I said, though, she ended up spending very little time here too far from the action. A peaceful life by the sea was not her idea of fun.'

Lesley wondered what it must be like to nip out at lunchtime and buy a villa by the sea for no better reason than *you could.* 'Is your mother-in-law expecting me?'

'No,' Alessio admitted. 'As far as Claudia is concerned, I am here on a mission to take my wayward daughter in hand and bring her back with me to London. I thought it best to keep the unsavoury details of this little visit to myself.' He leaned across to flip open the passenger door. 'I didn't think,' he continued, 'That

Rachel would have appreciated her grandmother knowing the ins and outs of what has been going on. Right. Let's get this over and done with.'

Lesley felt for him. Underneath the cool, composed exterior she knew that he would be feeling a certain dread at the conversation he would need to have with his daughter. He would be the Big, Bad Wolf and, for a sixteen-year-old, there would be no extenuating circumstances.

The ringing of the doorbell reverberated from the bowels of the villa. Just when Lesley thought that no one was in despite the abundance of lights on, she heard the sound of footsteps, and then the door was opening and there in front of them was a diminutive, timid looking woman in her mid-sixties: dark hair, dark, anxious eyes and a face that looked braced for an unpleasant surprise until she registered who was at the door and the harried expression broke into a beaming smile.

Lesley faded back, allowing for a rapid exchange of Italian, and only when there was a lull in the conversation did Claudia register her presence.

Despite what Alessio had said, Lesley had expected someone harder, tougher and colder. Her daughter, after all, had not come out of Alessio's telling of the story as an exemplary character, but now she could see why he had dismissed Claudia's ability to cope with Rachel.

Their arrival had been unannounced; they certainly had not been expected for supper. Alessio had been vague, Claudia told her, gripping Lesley's arm as she led them towards one of myriad rooms that comprised the ground floor of the ornately decorated house.

'I was not even sure that he would be coming at all,' she confided. 'Far less that he would be bringing a lady friend with him...'

Caught uncomfortably on the outside of a conversation she couldn't understand, Lesley could only smile weakly as Alessio fired off something in Italian and then they were entering the dining room where, evidently, dinner had been interrupted.

Standing a little behind both Claudia and Alessio, Lesley nervously looked around the room, feeling like an intruder in this strange family unit.

For a house by the coast, it was oddly furnished with ornate, dark wooden furniture, heavy drapes and a patterned rug that obscured most of the marble floor. Dominating one of the walls was a huge portrait of a striking woman with voluptuous dark good looks, wild hair falling over one shoulder and a haughty expression. Lesley assumed that it was Bianca and she could see why a boy of eighteen would have been instantly drawn to her.

The tension in the room was palpable. Claudia had bustled forward, but her movements were jerky and her smile was forced, while Alessio remained where he was, eyes narrowed, looking at the girl who had remained seated and was returning his stare with open insolence.

Rachel looked older than sixteen but then Lesley knew by now that she was only a few weeks away from her seventeenth birthday.

The tableau seemed to remain static for ages, even though it could only have been a matter of seconds. Claudia had launched into Italian and Rachel was pointedly ignoring her, although her gaze had shifted from Alessio, and now she was staring at Lesley with the concentration of an explorer spotting a new sub-species for the first time.

'And who are *you*?' She tossed her hair back, a mane of long, dark hair similar to the woman's in the portrait, although the resemblance ended there. Rachel had her father's aristocratic good looks. This was the gangly teenager whose leather mini-skirt Lesley had stealthily tried on. She reminded Lesley of the cool kids who had ruled the school as teenagers, except now a much older and more mature Lesley could see her for what she really was: a confused kid with a lot of attitude and a need to be defensive. She was scared of being hurt.

'Claudia.' Alessio turned to the older woman. 'If you would excuse us, I need to have a quiet word with my daughter.'

Claudia looked relieved and scuttled off, shutting the door quietly behind her.

Immediately Rachel launched into Italian and Alessio held up one commanding hand.

'English!'

It was the voice of complete and utter authority and his daughter glared at him, sullenly defiant but not quite brave enough to defy him.

'I'm Lesley.' Lesley moved forward into the simmering silence, not bothering to extend a hand in greeting because she knew it wouldn't be taken, instead sitting at the dining room table where she saw that Rachel had been playing a game on her phone.

'I helped to create that.' She pointed to the game with genuine pleasure. 'Three years ago.' She dumped the backpack onto the ground. 'I was seconded out to help design a website for a starter computer company and I got involved with the gaming side of things. It made a nice change. If I had only known how big that game would have become, I would have insisted on putting my name to it and then I would be getting royalties.'

Rachel automatically switched off the phone and turned it upside down.

Alessio had strolled towards his daughter and adopted the chair next to her so that she was now sandwiched between her father and Lesley.

'I know why you've come.' Rachel addressed her father in perfect, fluent English. 'And I'm not going back to England. I'm not going back to that stupid boarding school. I hate it there and I hate living with you. I'm staying here. Grandma Claudia said she's happy to have me.'

'I'm sure,' Alessio said in a measured voice, 'That you would love nothing more than to stay with your grandmother, running wild and doing whatever you want, but it is not going to happen.'

'You can't make me!'

Alessio sighed and raked his fingers through his hair. 'You're still a minor. I think you will find that I can.'

Looking between them, Lesley wondered if either realised just how alike they were: the proud jut of their chins, their stubbornness, even their mannerisms. Two halves of the same coin waiting to be aligned.

'I don't intend to have a protracted argument with you about this, Rachel. Returning to England is inevitable. We are both here because there is something else that needs to be discussed.'

He was the voice of stern authority and Lesley sighed as she reached down to the backpack and began extracting her folder, which she laid on the shiny table.

'What's that?' But her voice was hesitant under the defiance.

'A few weeks ago,' Alessio said impassively, 'I started getting emails. Lesley came to help me unravel them.'

Rachel was staring at the folder. Her face had paled and Lesley saw that she was gripping the arms of the chair. Impulsively she reached out and covered the thin, brown hand with hers and surprisingly it was allowed to remain there.

'It's thanks to me,' she said quietly, 'That all this stuff was uncovered. I'm afraid I looked through your bedroom. Your father, of course, would have rather I didn't, but it was the only way to compile the full picture.'

'You looked *through my things*?' Dark eyes were now focused accusingly on her, turned from Alessio. Lesley had become the target for Rachel's anger and confusion and Lesley breathed a little sigh of relief because, the less hostility directed at Alessio, the greater the chance of him eventually repairing his relationship with his daughter. It was worth it.

It was worth it because she loved him.

That realisation, springing out at her from nowhere, should have knocked her for six, but hadn't she already arrived that conclusion somewhere deep inside her? Hadn't she known that, underneath the arguments about lust and learning curves, stepping out of comfort zones and finding her sexuality, the simple truth of the matter was that she had been ambushed by the one thing she had never expected? It had struck her like a lightning bolt, penetrating straight through logic and common sense and obliterating her defences.

'You had no right,' Rachel was hissing.

Lesley let it wash over her and eventually the vitriol fizzled out and there was silence.

'So, tell me,' Alessio said in a voice that brooked no argument, 'About a certain Jack Perkins.'

Lesley left them after the initial setting out of the information. It was a sorry story of a lonely teenager, unhappy at boarding school, who had fallen in with the wrong crowd—or, rather, fallen in with the wrong boy. Piecing together the slips of paper and the stray emails, Lesley could only surmise that she had smoked a joint or two and then, vulnerable, knowing that she would be expelled from yet another school, she had become captive to a sixteen-year-old lad with a serious drug habit.

The finer details, she would leave for Alessio to discover. In the meantime, not quite knowing what to do with herself, she went outside and tried to get her thoughts in order.

Where did she go from here? She had always been in control of her life; she had always been proud of the fact that she knew where she was heading. She hadn't stopped for a minute to think that something as crazy as falling in love could ever derail her plans because she had always assumed that she would fall in love with someone who slotted into her life without causing too much of a ripple. She hadn't been lying when she had told Alessio that the kind of guy she imagined for herself would be someone very much like her.

How could she ever have guessed that the wrong person would come along and throw everything into chaos?

And what did she do now?

Still thinking, she felt rather than saw Alessio behind her and she turned around. Even in the darkness he had the bearing of a man carrying the weight of the world on his shoulders, and she instinctively walked towards him and wrapped her arms around his waist.

Alessio felt like he could hold onto her for ever. Wrong-footed by the intensity of that feeling, he pulled her closer and covered her mouth with his. His hand crept up underneath the tee-shirt and Lesley stepped back.

'Is sex the *only* thing you ever think about?' she

asked sharply, and she answered the question herself, providing the affirmative she knew was the death knell to any relationship they had.

He wanted sex, she wanted more—it was as simple as that. Never had the gulf between them seemed so vast. It went far beyond the differences in their backgrounds, their life experiences or their expectations. It was the very basic difference between someone who wanted love and someone who only wanted sex.

'How is Rachel?' She folded her arms, making sure to keep some space between them.

'Shaken.'

'Is that all you have to say? That she's *shaken*?'

'Are you deliberately trying to goad me into an argument?' Alessio looked at her narrowly. 'I'm frankly not in the mood to soothe whatever feathers I've accidentally ruffled.' He shook his head, annoyed with himself for venting his stress on her, but he had picked something up—something stirring under the surface—even though, for the life of him, he couldn't understand what could possibly be bugging her. She certainly hadn't spent the past hour trying and failing to get through to a wayward teenager who had sat in semi-mute silence absorbing everything that was being said to her but responding to nothing.

He was frustrated beyond endurance and he wondered if his own frustration was making him see nuances in her behaviour that weren't there.

'And I'm frankly amazed that you could talk to your daughter, have this awkward conversation, and yet have so little to report back on the subject.'

'I didn't realise that it was my duty to *report back* to you,' Alessio grated and Lesley reddened.

'Wrong choice of words.' She sighed. Here were the

cracks, she thought with a hollow sense of utter dejection. Things would go swimmingly well just so long as she could disentangle sex from love, but she was finding that she couldn't now. She spiked her fingers through her short hair and looked away from him, out towards the same black sea which his villa down the road overlooked.

She could see the way this would play out: making love would become a bittersweet experience; she would be the temporary mistress, making do, wondering when her time would be up. She suspected that that time would come very quickly once they returned to England. The refreshing, quirky novelty of bedding a woman with brains, who spoke her mind, who could navigate a computer faster than he could, would soon pall and he would begin itching to return to the unchallenging women who had been his staple diet.

Nor would he want a woman around who reminded him of the sore topic of his daughter and her misbehaviour, which had almost cost him a great deal of money.

'Would it be okay if I went to talk to her?' Lesley asked, and Alessio looked at her in surprise.

'What would you hope to achieve?'

'It might help talking to someone who isn't you.'

'Even though she sees you as the perpetrator of the "searching the bedroom" crime? I should have stepped in there and told her that that was a joint decision.'

'Why?' Lesley asked with genuine honesty. 'I guess you had enough on your plate to deal with and, besides, I will walk away from this and never see either of you again. If she pins the blame on me, then I can take it.'

Alessio's jaw hardened but he made no comment. 'She's still in the dining room,' he said. 'At least, that's where I left her. Claudia has disappeared to bed, and frankly I don't blame her. In the morning, I shall tell her that my daughter has agreed that the best thing is to return to England with me.'

'And school?'

'As yet to be decided, but it's safe to say that she won't be returning to her old stamping ground.'

'That's good.' She fidgeted, feeling his distance and knowing that, while she had been responsible for creating it, she still didn't like it. 'I won't be long,' she promised, and backed away.

Like a magnet, his presence seemed to want to pull her back towards him but she forced herself through to the dining room, little knowing what she would find.

She half-expected Rachel to have disappeared into another part of the house, but the teenager was still sitting in the same chair, staring vacantly through the window.

'I thought we might have a chat,' Lesley said, approaching her warily and pulling a chair out to sit right next to her.

'What for? Have you decided that you want to apologise for going through my belongings when *you had no right*?'

'No.'

Rachel looked at her sullenly. She switched on her mobile phone, switched it off again and rested it on the table.

'Your dad's been worried sick.'

'I'm surprised he could take the time off to be worried,' Rachel muttered, fiddling with the phone and then eventually folding her arms and looking at Lesley with unmitigated antagonism. 'This is all your fault.'

'Actually, it's got nothing to do with me. I'm only

here because of you and you're in this position because of what you did.'

'I don't have to sit here and listen to some stupid employee preach to me.' But she remained on the chair, glaring.

'And I don't have to sit here, but I want to, because I grew up without a mum and I know it can't be easy for you.'

'Oh puh…lease….' She dragged that one word out into a lengthy, disdainful, childish snort of contempt.

'Especially,' Lesley persevered, 'As Alessio—your father—isn't the easiest person in the world when it comes to touchy-feely conversations.'

'*Alessio*? Since when are you on first-name terms with my father?'

'He wants nothing more than to have a relationship with you, you know,' Lesley said quietly. She wondered if this was what love did, made you want to do your utmost to help the object of your affections, to make sure they were all right, even if you knew that they didn't return your love and would happily exit your life without much of a backward glance.

'And that's why he never bothered to get in touch when I was growing up? *Ever*?'

Lesley's heart constricted. 'Is that what you really believe?'

'It's what I was told by my mum.'

'I think you'll find that your father did his best to keep in touch, to visit… Well, you'll have to talk to him about that.'

'I'm not going to be talking to him again.'

'Why didn't you come clean with your dad, or even one of the teachers, when that boy started threatening you?' She had found a couple of crumpled notes and had quickly got the measure of a lad who had been happy to extort as much of Rachel's considerable pocket money as he could by holding it over her head that he had proof of the one joint she had smoked with him and was willing to lie to everyone that it had been more than that. When the pocket money had started running out, he must have decided to go directly to the goose that was laying the golden eggs: pay up or else he would go to the press and disclose that one of the biggest movers and shakers in the business world had a druggie teenage daughter. 'You must have been scared stiff,' she mused, half to herself.

'That's none of your business.'

Some of the aggression had left her voice. When Lesley looked at her, she saw the teenage girl who had been bullied and threatened by someone willing to take advantage of her one small error of judgement.

'Well, you dad's going to sort all of that out. He'll make the whole thing go away.' She heard the admiring warmth in her voice and cleared her throat. 'You should give him a chance.'

'And what's it to you?'

Lesley blushed.

'Oh, right.' She gave a knowing little laugh and sniffed. 'Well, I'm not about to give anyone a chance, and I don't care if he sorts that thing out or not. So. He dumped me and I had to traipse around with my mum and all her boyfriends.'

'You *knew* your mum…err…? Well, none of my business.' She stood up. 'You should give your dad a chance and at least listen to what he has to say. He tried very hard to keep in touch with you but, well, you should let him explain how that went—and you should go get some sleep.'

She exited the room, closing the door quietly behind her. Had she got through to Rachel? Who knew? It would take more than one conversation to break down some of those teenage walls, but several things had emerged.

Aside from the fact that everything was now on the table—and, whether she admitted it or not, that would have come as a huge relief to Rachel—it was clear that the girl had had no idea just how hard her father had tried to keep in touch with her, how hard he had fought to maintain contact.

And Alessio had no idea that his daughter was aware of Bianca's wild, promiscuous temperament.

Join those two things together, throw into the mix the fact that Rachel had kept a scrapbook of photos and cuttings, and Lesley suspected that an honest conversation between father and daughter would go some distance to opening the door to a proper relationship.

And if Rachel was no longer at a boarding school, but at a day school in London, they would both have the opportunity to start building a future and leaving the past behind.

She went outside to find Alessio still there and she quietly told him what she had learned during the conversation with his daughter.

'She thinks you abandoned her,' she reinforced bluntly. 'And she would have been devastated at the thought of that. It might explain why she's been such a rebel, but she's young. You're going to have to take the lead and lower your defences if you want to get through to her.'

Alessio listened, head tilted to one side, and when she had finished talking he nodded slowly and then told her in return what he intended to do to sort the small matter of a certain Jack Perkins. He had already contacted someone he trusted to supply him with information about the boy and he had enough at his disposal to pay a visit to his parents and make sure the matter was resolved quickly and efficiently, never again to rear its ugly head.

'When I'm through,' Alessio promised in a voice of steel, 'That boy will think twice before he goes near an Internet café again, never mind threatening anyone.'

Lesley believed him and she didn't doubt that Jack Perkins' life of crime was about to come crashing down around his head. It had transpired that his family was well-connected. Not only would they be horrified at what their son had done, and the drug problems he was experiencing, but his father would know that Alessio's power stretched far; if he were to be crossed again by a delinquent boy, then who knew what the repercussions would be?

The problem, Alessio assured her, would wait until he returned to the UK. It wasn't going anywhere and, whilst he could hand over the business of wrapping it up to a trusted advisor and friend, he would much rather do it himself.

'When I'm attacked,' he said softly, 'Then I prefer to retaliate using my own fists rather than relying on my bodyguards.'

Everything, Lesley thought, had been neatly wrapped up and she was certain that father and daughter would eventually find their way and become the family unit they deserved to be.

Which left her…the spectator whose purpose had been served and whose time had come to depart.

They drove in silence back to Alessio's villa. He planned on returning to his mother-in-law's the following morning and he would talk to his daughter once again.

He didn't say what that conversation would be, but Lesley knew that he had taken on board what she had said, and he would try and grope his way to some sort of mutual ground on which they could both converse.

Alessio knew that, generally speaking, the outcome to what could have been a disaster had been good.

Jack Perkins had revealed problems with his daughter that would now be addressed, and Lesley's mediation had been pretty damn fantastic. How could his daughter not have known that he had tried his hardest? He would set her straight on that. He could see that Rachel had been lost and therefore far too vulnerable in a school that had clearly allowed too much freedom. He might or might not take them to task on that.

'Thanks,' he suddenly said gruffly as they pulled up into the carport at the side of the villa. He killed the engine and looked at Lesley. 'You didn't just sort out who was behind this but you went the extra mile, and we both know, gentle bribe or no gentle bribe, you didn't have to do that.' Right now, all he wanted to do was get inside the villa, carry her upstairs to the bedroom and make love to her. Take all night making love to her. He had never felt as close to any woman.

No, Lesley thought with a tinge of bitterness, she really had had no need to go the extra mile, but she had, and it had had nothing to do with bribes, gentle or otherwise.

'We should talk,' she said after a while.

Alessio stilled. 'I thought we just had.'

Lesley hopped out of the car, slammed the door behind her and waited for him. Just then, in the car, it had felt way too intimate. Give it just a few more seconds sitting there, breathing him in, hearing that lazy, sexy drawl, and all her good intentions would have gone down the drain.

'Want to tell me what this is all about?' was the first thing he asked the second they were inside his villa. He threw the car keys on the hand-carved sideboard by the front door and led the way into the kitchen where he helped himself to a long glass of water from a bottle in the fridge. Then he sat down and watched as she took the seat furthest away from him.

'How long,' she finally asked, 'Do you plan on staying here?'

'Where is that question leading?' For the first time, he could feel quicksand underneath his feet and he didn't like it. He wished he had had something stronger to drink; a whisky would have gone down far better than a glass of water. He didn't like the way she had sat a million miles across the room from him; he didn't like the mood she had been in for the past few hours; he didn't like the way she couldn't quite seem to meet his eyes. 'Oh, for God's sake,' he muttered when she didn't say anything. 'At least until the end of the week. Rachel and I have a few things to sort out, not to mention a frank discussion of where she will go to school. There are a lot of fences to be mended and they won't be mended overnight; it'll take a few days before we can even work out where the holes are. But what has that got to do with anything?'

'I won't be staying on here with you.' She cleared her throat and took a deep breath. 'I do realise that I promised I would stay the week, but I think my job here is done, and it's time for me to return to London.'

'Your job here *is done*?' Alessio could not believe what he was hearing.

'Yes, and I just want to say that there's every chance that you and your daughter will find a happy solution to the difficulties you've been experiencing in your relationship.'

'Your job here...*is done*? So you're *heading back*?'

'I don't see the point of staying on.'

'And I don't believe I'm hearing this. What do you mean you don't *see the point of staying on*?' He point-blank refused to ask *what about us?* That was not a question that would ever pass his lips. He remembered what she had said about wanting to head back out there, get into the thick of the dating scene—now that she had used him to reintroduce her to the world of sex; now that she had overcome her insecurities, thanks to him.

Pride slammed in and he looked at her coldly.

'What we have, Alessio, isn't going anywhere. We both agreed on that, didn't we?' She could have kicked herself for the plaintive request she heard in her voice, the request begging him to contradict her. 'And I'm not interested in having a fling until we both run out of steam. Actually, probably until we get back to London. I'm not in the market for a holiday romance.'

'And what are you in the market for?' Alessio asked softly.

Lesley tilted her chin and returned his cool stare. Was she about to reveal that she was in the market for a long-term, for ever, happy-ever-after, committed relationship? Would she say that so that he could naturally assume that she was talking about *him*? Wanting that relationship *with him*? It would be the first conclusion he would reach. Women, he had told her, always seemed to want more than he was prepared to give. He would assume that she had simply joined the queue.

There was no way that she would allow her dignity to be trampled into the ground.

'Right now...' her voice was steady and controlled, giving nothing away '...all I want is to further my career. The company is still growing. There are loads of opportunities to grow with it, even perhaps to be transferred to another part of the country. I want to be there to take advantage of those opportunities.' She thought she sounded like someone trying to sell themselves at an interview, but she held her ground and her eyes remained clear and focused.

'And the career opportunities are going to disappear unless you hurry back to London as fast as you can?'

'I realise you'll probably pull that big job out from under our feet.' That thought only now struck her, as did the conclusion that she wasn't going to win employee of the week if her boss found out that she had been instrumental in losing a job that would bring hundreds of thousands of pounds to the company and extend their reach far wider than they had anticipated.

Alessio wondered whether her thirst for a rewarding career would make her change her mind about not staying on, about not continuing what they had. It revolted him to think that it might. He had never had to use leverage to get any woman into his bed and he wasn't about to start now.

Nor had he ever had to beg any woman to stay in his bed once she was there, and he certainly wasn't about to start *that* now.

'You misjudge me,' he said coldly. 'I offered that job to your boss and I am not a man who would renege on a promise, least of all over an affair that goes belly up. Your company has the job and everything that goes with it.'

Lesley lowered her eyes. He was a man of honour. She had known that. He just wasn't a man in love.

'I also think that when I decide to embark on another relationship.'

'You mean after you've launched yourself back into the singles scene.'

She shrugged, allowing him to think something she knew to be way off mark. She could think of nothing less likely than painting the town red and clubbing.

'I just feel that, if I decide to get involved with anyone, then it should be with the person who is right for me. So, I think we should call it a day for us.'

'Good luck with your search,' Alessio gritted. 'And, now that you've said your piece, I shall go and do some work downstairs. Feel free to use the bedroom where your suitcase has been put; I shall sleep in one of the other bedrooms and you can book your return flight first thing in the morning. Naturally, I will cover the cost.' He stood up and walked towards the door. 'I intend to go to Claudia's by nine tomorrow. If I don't see you before I go, have a safe flight. The money I owe you will be in your bank account by the time you land.' He nodded curtly and shut the kitchen door behind him.

This is all for the best, Lesley thought, staring at the closed door and trying to come to terms with the thought that she would probably never see him again.

It was time for her to move on…

CHAPTER NINE

LESLEY PAUSED IN front of the towering glass house and stared up and up and up. Somewhere in there, occupying three floors in what was the most expensive office block in central London, Alessio would be hard at work. At least, she hoped so. She hoped he wasn't out of the country. She didn't think she could screw up her courage and make this trip to see him a second time.

A month ago, she had walked out on him and she hadn't heard from him since. Not a word. He had duly deposited a wad of money into her account, as he had promised—far too much, considering she had bailed on their trip a day in.

How had his talk with his daughter turned out? Had they made amends, begun the protracted process of repairing their relationship? Where was she at school now?

Had he found someone else? Had he found her replacement?

For the past few weeks, those questions had churned round and round in her head, buzzing like angry hornets, growing fat on her misery until… Well, until something else had come along that was so big and so overwhelming that there was no room left in her head for those questions.

She took a deep breath and propelled her reluctant feet forward until she was standing in the foyer of the building, surrounded by a constant river of people coming and going, some in snappy suits, walking with an air of purpose; others, clearly tourists, staring around them, wondering where they should go to get to the viewing gallery or to one of the many restaurants.

In front of her a long glass-and-metal counter separated a bank of receptionists from the public. They each had a snazzy, small computer screen in front of them and they were all impeccably groomed.

She had worked out what she was going to say, having decided beforehand that it wasn't going to be easy gaining access to the great Alessio Baldini—that, in fact, he might very well refuse to see her at all. She had formulated a borderline sob story, filled with innuendo and just enough of a suggestion that, should she not be allowed up to whatever floor he occupied, he would be a very angry man.

It worked. Ten minutes after she had arrived, a lift was carrying her up to one of the top floors, from which she knew he would be able to overlook all of London. She had no idea how much the rent was on a place like this and her head spun thinking about it. She had been told that she would be met at the lift, and she was, but it was only as they were approaching his office that nerves really truly kicked in and she had to fight to keep her breathing steady and even and not to hyperventilate.

She was aware of his personal assistant asking concerned questions and she knew that she was answering those questions in a reassuring enough voice, but she felt sick to the stomach.

By the time they reached his office suite, she was close to fainting.

She didn't even know if she was doing the right thing. The decision to come here had been taken and then rejected and then taken again so many times that she had lost count.

The outer office, occupied by his personal assistant, was luxurious. In one corner, a massive semi-circular desk housed several phones and a computer terminal. Against one of the walls was a long, grey bench-like sofa that looked very uncomfortable. Against the other wall was a smooth, walnut built-in cupboard with no handles, just a bank of smooth wood.

It was an intimidating office, but not as intimidating as the massive door behind which Alessio would be waiting for her.

And waiting for her he most certainly was. He had been in the middle of a conference call when he had been buzzed by his secretary and informed that a certain Lesley Fox was downstairs in reception and should she be sent away or brought up?

Alessio had cut short his conference call without any preamble. His better self had told him to refuse her entry. Why on earth would he want to have anything further to do with a woman who had slept with him, had not denied having slept with him as part of her preparations for entering the world of hectic dating and then walked out of his life without a backward glance? Why would he engage in any further conversation with someone who had made it perfectly clear that he was not the sort of man she was looking for, even though they had slept together? Even though there had been no complaints there!

He had made sure that the money owed to her was deposited into her bank account, and had had no word from her confirming whether she had received it or not, despite the fact that he had paid her over and above the agreed amount, including paying her for time she had not worked for him at all.

The time he had wasted waiting for a phone call or text from her had infuriated him.

Not to mention the time he had wasted just *thinking* about her. She was hardly worth thinking about and yet, in the past few weeks, she had been on his mind like a background refrain he just couldn't get out of his head.

And so, when he had been called on his internal line to be told that she was there in the building, that she wanted to see him, there had been no contest in his head.

He had no idea what she could possibly want, and underwriting his curiosity was the altogether pleasant day dream that she had returned to beg for him back. Perhaps the wild and wonderful world of chatting up random men in bars and clubs had not quite lived up to expectation. Maybe having fun with the wrong guy was not quite the horror story she had first thought. Maybe she missed the sex; she had certainly seemed to enjoy every second of being touched by him.

Or, more prosaically, maybe her boss had sent her along on something to do with the job he had put their way. It made sense. She knew him. Indeed, they had landed that lucrative contract without even having to tender for it because of her. If anything needed to be discussed, her boss would naturally assume that she should be the one to do it and there would be no way that she could refuse. At least, not unless she started pouring out the details of her private life, which he knew she would never do.

He frowned, not caring for that scenario, which he immediately jettisoned so that he could focus as he waited for her on more pleasurable ones.

By the time his secretary, Claire, announced her arrival, through the internal line to which she exclusively had access, Alessio had come to the conclusion that he was only mildly curious as to the nature of her surprise visit—that he didn't care a whit what she had to say to him and that the only reason he was even allowing her entry into his office was because he was gentlemanly enough not to have her chucked out from the foyer in full view of everyone.

Still, he made her wait a while, before sitting back in his leather chair and informing Claire that his visitor could be ushered in—cool, calm and screamingly forbidding.

Lesley felt the breath catch jaggedly in her throat as she heard the door close quietly behind her. Of course, she hadn't forgotten what he looked like. How could she when his image had been imprinted in her brain with the red-hot force of a branding iron?

But nothing had prepared her for the cold depths of those dark eyes or the intimidating silence that greeted her arrival in his office.

She didn't know whether to keep standing or to confidently head for one of the leather chairs in front of his desk so that she could sit down. She certainly felt as though her legs didn't have much strength left in them.

Eventually, she only scuttled towards one of the chairs when he told her to sit, simultaneously glancing at his watch as though to remind her that, whilst she might have been offered a seat, she should make sure that she didn't get too comfortable because he didn't have a lot of time for her.

This was the guy she had fallen in love with. She knew she would have dented his pride when she had walked out on him, but still she had half-hoped that he might contact her in some way, if only to ask whether she had received the money he had deposited into her account.

Or else to fill her in on what had happened in his family drama. Surely that would have been the polite thing to do?

But not a word, and she knew that had she not arrived on his doorstep, so to speak, then she would never have seen him again. Right now, those brooding dark eyes were surveying her with all the enthusiasm of someone contemplating something the cat had inadvertently brought in.

'So,' Alessio finally drawled, tapping his rarely used fountain pen on the surface of his desk. 'To what do I owe this unexpected pleasure?' To his disgust, he couldn't help but think that she looked amazing.

He had made one half-hearted attempt to replace her with one of the women he had dated several months ago, a hot blonde with big breasts and a face that could turn heads from a mile away, but he had barely been able to stick it out for an evening in her company.

How could he when he had been too busy thinking of the woman slumped in the chair in front of him? Not in her trademark jeans this time but a neat pair of dark trousers and a snug little jacket that accentuated the long, lean lines of her body.

On cue, he felt himself begin to respond, which irritated the hell out of him.

'I'm sorry if I'm disturbing you,' Lesley managed. Now that she was here, she realised that she couldn't just drop her bombshell on him without any kind of warning.

'I'm a busy man.' He gesticulated widely and shot her a curving smile that contained no warmth. 'But never let it be said that I'm rude. An ex-lover deserves at least a few minutes of my time.'

Lesley bit her tongue and refrained from telling him that that remark in itself was the height of rudeness.

'I won't be long. How is Rachel?'

'You made this journey to talk about my daughter?'

Lesley shrugged. 'Well, I became quite involved in what was going on. I'm curious to know how things turned out in the end.'

Alessio was pretty sure that she hadn't travelled to central London and confronted him at his office just to ask one or two questions about Rachel, but he was willing to play along with the game until she revealed the true reason for showing up.

'My daughter has been…subdued since this whole business came out in the open. She returned to London without much fuss and she seems relieved that the boarding school option is now no longer on the cards. Naturally, I have had to lay down some ground rules for her—the most important of which is that I don't want to hear from anyone in the school that she's been acting up.' Except he had been far less harsh in delivering that message than it sounded.

Rachel might have been a complete idiot, led astray for reasons that were fairly understandable, but he had to accept his fair share of the blame as well. He had taken his eye off the ball.

Now, there was dialogue between them, and he had high hopes that in time that dialogue would turn into fluent conversation. Would that be asking too much?

He had certainly taken the unfortunate affair by the horns and sorted it all out, personally paying a visit to the boy's parents and outlining for them in words of one syllable what would happen if he ever had another email from the lad.

He had shied away from taking the full hard line, however, confident that the boy's parents, who had seemed decent but bewildered, would take matters in hand. They both travelled extensively and only now had it dawned on them that in their absence they had left behind a lonely young man with a drug problem that had fortunately been caught in the bud.

Rachel had not commented on the outcome, but he had been shrewd enough to see the relief on her face. She had found herself caught up in something far bigger than she had anticipated and, in the end, he had come to her rescue, although that was something he had taken care not to ram home.

'That's good.' Lesley clasped her hands together.

'So is there anything else you want? Because if that's all…' He looked at the slender column of her neck, her down-bent head, the slump of her shoulders, and wanted to ask her if she missed him.

Where the hell had *that* notion come from?

'Just one other thing.' She cleared her throat and looked at him with visible discomfort.

And, all at once, Alessio knew where she was going with this visit of hers. She wanted back in with him. She had walked away with her head held high and a load of nonsense about needing to find the right guy, wherever the hell he might be. But, having begun her search, she had obviously fast reached the conclusion that the right guy wasn't going to be as easy to pin down as she had thought and, in the absence of Mr Right, Mr Fantastic Sex would do instead.

Over his dead body.

Although, it had to be said that the thought of her

begging for him was an appealing one. He turned that pleasant fantasy over in his head and very nearly smiled.

He was no longer looking at his watch. Instead, he pushed the chair away from the desk and relaxed back, his fingers lightly linked together on his flat, hard stomach.

Should he rescue her from the awkwardness of what she wanted to say? Or should he just wait in growing silence until her eventual discomfort propelled her into speech? Both options carried their own special appeal.

Eventually, with a rueful sigh that implied that far too much of his valuable time had already been wasted, he said, shaking his head, 'Sorry. It's a little too late for you.'

Lesley looked at him in sudden confusion. She knew that this was an awkward situation. She had appeared at his office and demanded to see him, and now here she was, body as stiff as a plank of wood, sitting in mute silence while she tried to work how best to say what she had come to say. No wonder he wanted to shuffle her out as fast as he could. He must be wondering what the hell she was doing, wasting his time.

'You're—you're busy,' she stammered, roused into speech as her brain sluggishly cranked back into gear just enough to understand that he wanted her out because he had more important things to do.

Once again, she wondered whether she had been replaced. Once again, she wondered whether he had reverted to type, back to the sexy blondes with the big breasts and the big hair.

'Have you been busy?' she blurted out impulsively, almost but not quite covering her mouth with her hand in an instinctive and futile attempt to retract her words.

Alessio got her drift immediately. No matter that the

question hadn't been completed. He could tell from the heightened colour in her cheeks and her startled, embarrassed eyes that she was asking him about his sex life, and he felt a groundswell of satisfaction.

'Busy? Explain.'

'Work. You know.' When she had thought about having this conversation, about seeing him again, she had underestimated the dramatic effect he would have on her senses. In her head, she had pictured herself cool, composed—a little nervous, understandably, but strong enough to say her piece and leave.

Instead, here she was, her thoughts all over the place and her body responding to him on that deep, subterranean level that was so disconcerting. The love which she had hoped might have found a more settled place—somewhere not to the forefront—pounded through her veins like a desperate virus, destroying everything in its path and making her stumble over her words.

Not to mention she'd hoped not to ask questions that should never have left her mouth, because she could tell from the knowing look in those deep, dark eyes that he knew perfectly well what she had wanted to know when she had asked him whether he had been 'busy'.

'Work's been…work. It's always busy. Outside of work…' Alessio thought of his non-date with a non-contender for a partner and felt his hackles rise that the woman staring at him with those big, almond-shaped brown eyes had driven him into seeking out someone for company simply to try and replace the images of her he had somehow ended up storing in his head. He shrugged, letting her assume that his private life was a delicate place to which she was not invited—hilarious, considering just how much she knew about him. 'What about you?' He smoothly changed the subject. 'Have you found your perfect soul-mate as yet?'

'What did you mean when you said that it was a little too late for me?' The remark had been playing at the back of her mind and she knew that she needed him to spell it out in words of one syllable.

'If you think that you can walk back into my life because you had a bit of trouble locating Mr Right, then it's not going to happen.'

Pride. But then, what the hell was wrong with pride? He certainly had no intention of telling her the truth, which was that he was finding it hard to rid his system of her, even though she should have been no more than a blurry memory by now.

He was a man who moved on when it came to women. Always had been—never mind when it came to moving on from a woman who had dumped him!

Just thinking about that made his teeth snap together in rage.

'I don't intend walking back into your life,' Lesley replied coolly. So, now she knew where she stood. Was she still happy that she had come here? Frankly, she could still turn around and walk right back through that door but, yes, she was happy she was here, whatever the outcome.

Alessio's eyes narrowed. He noticed what he had failed to notice before—the rigid way she was sitting, as though every nerve in her body was on red-hot alert; the way she was fiddling with her fingers; the determined tilt of her chin.

'Then why are you here?' His voice was brusque and dismissive. Having lingered on the pleasant scenario of her pleading to be a part of his life once again, he was irrationally annoyed that he had misread whatever signals she had been giving off.

'I'm here because I'm pregnant.'

There. She had said it. The enormous thing that had been absorbing every minute of every day of her life since she had done that home pregnancy test over three days ago was finally out in the open.

She had skipped a period. It hadn't even occurred to her that she could be pregnant; she had forgotten all about that torn condom. She had had far too much on her mind for that little detail to surface. It was only as she'd tallied the missed period with tender breasts that she remembered the very first time they had made love…and the outcome of that had been very clear to see in the bright blue line on that little plastic stick.

She hadn't bothered to buy more, to repeat the test. Why would she do that, when in her heart she knew that the result was accurate?

She had had a couple of days to get used to the idea, to move from feeling as though she was falling into a bottomless hole to gradually accepting that, whatever the landing, she would have to deal with it; that the hole wouldn't be bottomless.

She had had time to engage her brain in beginning trying to work out how her life would change, because there was no way that she would be getting rid of this baby. And, as her brain had engaged, her emotions had followed suit and a flutter of excitement and curiosity had begun to work their way into the equation.

She was going to be a mum. She hadn't banked on that happening, and she knew that it would bring a host of problems, but she couldn't snuff out that little flutter of excitement.

Boy or girl? What would it look like? A miniature

Alessio? Certainly, a permanent reminder of the only man she knew she would ever love.

And should she tell him? If she loved him, would she ruin his life by telling him that he was going to be a father—again? Another unplanned and unwanted pregnancy. Would he think that she was trapping him, just like Bianca had, into marriage for all the wrong reasons?

Wouldn't the kindest thing be to keep silent, to let him carry on with his life? It was hardly as though he had made any attempt at all to contact her after she had left Italy! She had been a bit of fun and he had been happy enough to watch her walk away. Wouldn't the best solution be to let him remember her as a bit of fun rather than detonate a bomb that would have far-reaching and permanent ramifications he would not want?

In the end, she just couldn't bring herself to deny him the opportunity of knowing that he was going to be a father. The baby was half his and he had his rights, whatever the outcome might be.

But it was still a bomb she'd detonated, and she could see that in the way his expression changed from total puzzlement to dawning comprehension and then to shock and horror.

'I'm sorry,' she said in a clear, high voice. 'I know this is probably the last thing you were expecting.'

Alessio was finding it almost impossible to join his thoughts up. Pregnant. She was pregnant. For once he couldn't find the right words to deal with what was going through his head, to express himself. In fact, he actually couldn't find any words at all.

'It was that first time,' Lesley continued into the lengthening silence. 'Do you remember?'

'The condom split.'

'It was a one in a thousand chance.'

'The condom split and now you're pregnant.' He leant forward and raked his fingers through his hair, keeping his head lowered.

'It was no one's fault,' Lesley said, chewing her lower lip and looking at his reaction, the way he couldn't even look at her. Right now he hated her; that was clear. He was listening to the sound of his life being derailed and, whether down to a burst condom or not, he was somehow blaming her.

'I wasn't going to come here…'

That brought his head up, snapping to attention, and he looked at her in utter disbelief. 'What, you were just going to disappear with my baby inside you and not tell me about it?'

'Can you blame me?' Lesley muttered defensively. 'I know the story about how you were trapped into a loveless marriage by your last wife; I know what the consequences of that were.'

'Those consequences being…?' When Bianca had smiled smugly and told him that he was going to be a father, he had been utterly devastated. Now, strangely, the thought that this woman might have spared him devastation second time round didn't sit right. In fact, he was furious that the thought might even have crossed her mind although, in some rational part of himself, he could fully understand why. He also knew the answer to his own stupid question, although he waited for her to speak while his thoughts continued to spin and spin, as though they were in a washing machine with the speed turned high.

'No commitment,' Lesley said without bothering to dress it up. 'No one ever allowed to get too close. No woman ever thinking that she could get her foot through the door, because you were always ready to bang that door firmly shut the minute you smelled any unwanted advances in that direction. And please don't look at me as though I'm talking rubbish, Alessio. We both know I'm not. So excuse me for thinking that it might have been an idea to spare you the nightmare of…of this…'

'So you would have just disappeared?' He held onto that tangible, unappealing thought and allowed his anger to build up. 'Walked away? And then what—in sixteen years' time I would have found out that I'd fathered a child when he or she came knocking on my door asking to meet me?'

'I hadn't thought that far into the future.' She shot him a mutinous look from under her lashes. 'I looked into a future a few months away and what I saw was a man who would resent finding himself trapped again.'

'You can't speculate on what my reactions might or might not have been.'

'Well, it doesn't matter. I'm here now. I've told you. And there's something else—I want you to know straight off that I'm not asking you for anything. You know the situation and that's my duty done.' She began standing up and found that she was trembling. Alessio stared at her with open-mouthed incredulity.

'Where do you think you're going?'

'I'm leaving.' She hesitated. This was the right time to leave. She had done what she had come to do. There was no way that she intended to put any pressure on him to do anything but carry on with his precious, loveless existence, free from the responsibility of a clinging woman and an unwanted baby.

Yet his presence continued to pull her towards him like a powerful magnet.

'You're kidding!' Alessio's voice cracked with the

harshness of a whip. 'You breeze in here, tell me that you're carrying my child, and then announce that you're on your way!'

'I told you, I don't want anything from you.'

'What you want is by the by.'

'I beg your pardon?'

'It's impossible having this sort of conversation here. We need to get out, go somewhere else. My place.'

Lesley stared at him in utter horror. Was he mad? The last thing she wanted was to be cooped up with him on his turf. It was bad enough that she was in his office. Besides, where else was the conversation going to go?

Financial contributions; of course. He was a wealthy man and in possession of a muddy conscience; he would salve it by flinging money at it.

'I realise you might want to help out on the money front,' she said stiltedly. 'But, believe it or not, that's not why I came here. I can manage perfectly well on my own. I can take maternity leave and anyway, with what I do, I should be able to work from home.'

'You don't seem to be hearing me.' He stood up and noticed how she fell back.

She might want him out of her life but it wasn't going to happen. Too bad if her joyful hunt for the right guy had crashed and burned; she was having his baby and he was going to be part of her life whether she liked it or not.

The thought was not as unwelcome as he might have expected. In fact, he was proud of how easily he was beginning to take the whole thing on board.

It made sense, of course. He was older and wiser. He had mellowed over time. Now that sick feeling of having an abyss yawn open at his feet was absent.

'If you want to discuss the financial side of things,

then we can do that at a later date. Right now, I'll give you time to digest everything.'

'I've digested it. Now, sit back down.' This was not where he wanted to be. An office couldn't contain him. He felt restless, in need of moving. He wanted the space of his apartment. But there was no way she would go there with him; he was astute enough to decipher that from her dismayed reaction to the suggestion. And he wasn't going to push it.

It crossed his mind that this might have come as a bolt from the blue for him, turning his life on its axis and sending it spiralling off in directions he could never have predicted, but it would likewise have been the same for her. Yet here she was, apparently in full control. But then, hadn't he always known that there was a thread of absolute bravery and determination running through her?

And when she said that she didn't want anything from him, he knew that she meant it. This situation could not have been more different from the one in which he had found himself all those years ago.

Not that that made any difference. He was still going to be a presence in her life now whether she liked it or not.

Lesley had reluctantly sat back down and was now looking at him with a sullen lack of enthusiasm. She had expected more of an explosion of rage, in the middle of which she could have sneaked off, leaving him to calm down. He seemed to be handling the whole thing a great deal more calmly than she had expected.

'This isn't just about me contributing to the mother and baby fund,' he said, in case she had got it into her head that it might be. 'You're having my baby and I intend to be involved in this every single step of the way.'

'What are you talking about?'

'Do you really take me for a man who walks away from responsibility?'

'I'm not your ex-wife!' Lesley said tightly, fists clenched on her lap. 'I haven't come here looking for anything and you certainly don't owe me or this baby anything!'

'I'm not going to be a part-time father,' Alessio gritted. 'I was a part-time father once, not of my own choosing, and it won't happen again.'

Not once had Lesley seen the situation from that angle. Not once had she considered that he would want actual, active involvement, yet it made perfect sense. 'What are you suggesting?' she asked, bewildered and on the back foot.

'What else is there to suggest but marriage?'

For a few frozen seconds, Lesley thought that she might have misheard him, but when she looked at him his face was set, composed and unyielding.

She released a hysterical laugh that fizzled out very quickly. 'I don't believe I'm hearing this. Are you mad? Get married?'

'Why so shocked?'

'Because…' *Because you don't love me. You probably don't even like me very much right now.* 'Because having a baby isn't the right reason for two people to get married,' she said in as controlled a voice as she could muster. 'You of all people should know that! Your marriage ended in tears because you went into it for all the wrong reasons.'

'Any marriage involving my ex-wife would have ended in tears.' Alessio was finding it hard to grapple with the notion that she had laughed at his suggestion of marriage. Was she *that* intent on finding Mr Right that she couldn't bear the thought of being hitched to him? It was downright offensive! 'You're not Bianca, and you need to look at the bigger picture.' Was that overly aggressive? He didn't think so but he saw the way she stiffened and he tempered what he was going to say with a milder, more conciliatory voice. 'By which I mean that this isn't about us as individuals but about a child that didn't ask to be brought into the world. To do the best for him or her is to provide a united family.'

'To do the best for him or her is to provide two loving parents who live separately instead of two resentful ones joined in a union where there's no love lost.' Just saying those words out loud made her feel ill because what she should really have said was that there was no worse union than one in which love was given but not returned. What she could have told him was that she could predict any future where they were married, and what she could see was him eventually loathing her for being the other half of a marriage he might have initiated but which had eventually become his prison cell.

There was a lot she could have told him but instead all she said was, 'There's no way I would ever marry you.'

CHAPTER TEN

THE PAIN STARTED just after midnight. Five months before her due date. Lesley awoke, at first disorientated, then terrified when, on inspection, she realised that she was bleeding.

What did that mean? She had read something about that in one of the many books Alessio had bought for her. Right now, however, her brain had ceased to function normally. All she could think of doing was getting on her mobile phone and calling him.

She had knocked him back, had told him repeatedly that she wasn't going to marry him, yet he had continued to defy her low expectations by stealthily becoming a rock she could lean on. He was with her most evenings, totally disregarding what she had said to him about pregnancy not being an illness. He had attended the antenatal appointments with her. He had cunningly incorporated Rachel into the picture, bringing his daughter along with him many of the times he'd visited her, talking as though the future held the prospect of them all being a family, even though Lesley had been careful to steer clear of agreeing to any such sweeping statements.

What was he hoping to achieve? She didn't know. He didn't love her and not once had he claimed to.

But, bit by bit, she knew that she was beginning to rely on him—and it was never so strongly proved as now, when the sound of his deep voice over the end of the phone had the immediate effect of calming her panicked nerves.

'I should have stayed the night,' was the first thing he told her, having made it over to her house in record time.

'It wasn't necessary.' Lesley leaned back and closed her eyes. The pain had diminished but she was still in a state of shock at thinking that something might be wrong. That she might lose the baby. Tears threatened close to the surface but she pushed them away, focusing on a good outcome, despite the fact that she knew she was still bleeding.

And then something else occurred to her, a wayward thought that needled its way into her brain and took root, refusing to budge. 'I shouldn't have called you,' she said more sharply than she had intended. 'I wouldn't have if I'd thought that you were going to fret and worry.' But she hadn't thought of doing anything *but* picking up that phone to him. To a man who had suddenly become indispensable despite the fact that she was not the love of his life; despite the fact that he wouldn't be in this car here with her now if she had never visited him in his office.

She had never foreseen the way he had managed to become so ingrained into the fabric of her daily life. He brought food for her. He stocked her up with pregnancy books. He insisted they eat in when he was around because it was less hassle than going out. He had taken care of that persistent leak in the bathroom which had suddenly decided to act up.

And not once had she sat back and thought of where all this was leading.

'Of course you should have called me,' Alessio said softly. 'Why wouldn't you? This baby is mine as well. I share all the responsibilities with you.'

And share them he had, backing away from trying to foist his marriage solution onto her, even though he had been baffled at her stubborn persistence that there was no way that she was going to marry him.

Why not? He just didn't get it. They were good together. They were having a baby. Hell, he had made sure not to lay a finger on her, but he still burned to have her in his bed, and the memory of the sex they had shared still made him lose concentration in meetings. And, yes, so maybe he had mentioned once or twice that he had learnt bitter lessons from being trapped into marriage by the wrong woman for the wrong reasons, but hadn't that made his proposal even more sincere—the fact that he was willing to sidestep those unfortunate lessons and re-tread the same ground?

Why couldn't she see that?

He had stopped thinking about the possibility that she was still saving herself for Mr Right. Just going down that road made him see red.

'I hate it when you talk about responsibilities,' she snapped, looking briefly at him and then just as quickly looking away. 'And you're driving way too fast. We're going to crash.'

'I'm sticking to the speed limit. Of course I'm going to talk about responsibilities. Why shouldn't I?' Would she rather he had turned his back on her and walked away? Was that the sort of modern guy she would have preferred him to be? He hung onto his patience with difficulty, recognising that the last thing she needed was to be stressed out.

'I just want you to know,' Lesley said fiercely, 'That if anything happens to this baby…'

'Nothing is going to happen to this baby.'

'You don't know that!'

Alessio could sense her desire to have an argument with him and he had no intention of allowing her to indulge that desire. A heated row was not appropriate but he shrewdly guessed that, if he mentioned that, it would generate an even bigger row.

What the hell was wrong? Of course she was worried. So was he, frankly. But he was here with her, driving her to the hospital, fully prepared to be right there by her side, so why the need to launch into an attack?

Frustration tore into him but, like his impatience, he kept it firmly in check.

Suddenly she felt that it was extremely important that she let him know this vital thing. 'And I just want you to know that, if something does, then your duties to me are finished. You can walk away with a clear conscience, knowing that you didn't dump me when I was pregnant with your child.'

Alessio sucked in his breath sharply. Ahead, he could see the big, impersonal hospital building. He had wanted her to have private medical care during the pregnancy and for the birth of the baby, but she had flatly refused, and he had reluctantly ceded ground. If, indeed, there was anything at all amiss, that small victory would be obliterated because he would damn well make sure that she got the best medical attention there was available.

'This is not the time for this sort of conversation.' He screeched to a halt in front of the Accident and Emergency entrance but, before he killed the engine, he looked at her intently, his eyes boring into her. 'Just try and relax, my darling. I know you're probably scared stiff but I'm here for you.' He brushed her cheek lightly and the tenderness of that touch brought a lump to her throat.

'You're here for the baby, not for me,' Lesley muttered under her breath. But then any further conversation was lost as they were hurried through, suddenly caught up in a very efficient process, channelled to the right place, speeding along the quiet hospital corridors with Lesley in a wheelchair and Alessio keeping pace next to her.

There seemed to be an awful lot of people around and she clasped his hand tightly, hardly even realising that she was doing that.

'If something happens to the baby…' he bent to whisper into her ear as they headed towards the ultrasound room '…then I'm still here for you.'

An exhausting hour later, during which Lesley had had no time to think about what those whispered words meant, she finally found herself in a private room decorated with a television on a bracket against the wall and a heavy door leading, she could see, to her own en-suite bathroom.

Part of her wondered whether those whispered words had actually been uttered or had they been a fiction of her fevered imagination?

She covertly watched as he drew the curtains together and then pulled a chair so that he was on eye-level with her as she lay on the bed.

'Thank you for bringing me here, Alessio,' she said with a weak smile that ended up in a yawn.

'You're tired. But everything's going to be all right with the baby. Didn't I say?'

Lesley smiled with her eyes half-closed. The relief

was overwhelming. They had pointed out the strongly beating heart on the scan and had reassured her that rest was all that was called for. She had been planning to work from home towards the beginning of the third trimester. That would now have to be brought forward.

'You said.'

'And—and I meant what I said when we were rushing you in.'

Lesley's eyes flew open and she felt as though her heart had skipped a beat. She had not intended to remind him of what he had said, just in case she had misheard, just in case he had said what he somehow thought she wanted to hear in the depths of her anxiety over her scare.

But now his eyes held hers and she just wanted to lose herself in possibilities.

'What did you say? I can't quite…um…remember.' She looked down at her hand which had somehow found its way between his much bigger hands.

'What I should say is that there was a moment back then when it flashed through my mind—what would I do if anything happened to *you*? It scared the living daylights out of me.'

'I know you feel very responsible…with me being pregnant.' She deliberately tried to kill the shoot of hope rising inside her and tenaciously refusing to go away.

'I'm not talking about the baby. I'm talking about you.' He felt as though he was looking over the side of a very sheer cliff, but he wanted to jump; he didn't care what sort of landing he might be heading for.

So far she hadn't tried to remind him that he wasn't her type and that they weren't suited for one another. That surely had to be a good sign?

'I don't know what I'd do if anything happened to

you because you're the love of my life. No, wait, don't say a thing. Just listen to what I have to say and then, if you want me to butt out of your life, I'll do as you say. We can go down the legal route and have the papers drawn up for custody rights, and an allowance to be made for you, and I'll stop pestering you with my attention.' He took a deep breath and his eyes shifted to her mouth, then to the unappealing hospital gown which she was still wearing, and then finally they settled on their linked fingers. It seemed safer.

'I'm listening.' *The love of his life*? She just wanted to repeat that phrase over and over in her head because she didn't think she could possibly get used to hearing it.

'When you first appeared at my front door, I knew you were different to every single woman I had ever met. I knew you were sharp, feisty, outspoken. I was drawn to you, and I guess the fact that you occupied a special place of intimate knowledge about certain aspects of my private life not usually open to public view fuelled my attraction. It was as though the whole package became irresistible. You were sexy as hell without knowing it. You had brains and you had insight into me.'

Lesley almost burst out laughing at the 'sexy as hell' bit but then she remembered the way he had looked at her when they had made love, the things he had said. *She* might have had insecurities about how she looked, but she didn't doubt that his attraction had been genuine and spontaneous. Hadn't he been the one to put those insecurities to bed, after all?

'It just felt so damned right between us,' he admitted, stealing a surreptitious look at her face, and encouraged that she didn't seem to be blocking him out. 'And the more we got to know one another the better it felt. I thought it was all about the sex, but it was much bigger than that, and I just didn't see it. Maybe after Bianca I simply assumed that women could only satisfy a certain part of me before they hit my metaphorical glass ceiling and disappeared from my life. I wasn't looking for any kind of involvement and I certainly didn't bank on finding any. But involvement found me without my even realising it.'

He laughed under his breath and, when he felt the touch of her hand on his cheek, he held it in place so that he could flip it over and kiss the palm of her hand. He relaxed, but not too much.

'Thanks to you, my relationship with Rachel is the healthiest it's ever been. Thanks to you, I've discovered that there's far more to life than trying to be a father to a hostile teenager and burying myself in my work. I never stopped to question how it was that I wasn't gutted when you told me about the pregnancy. I knew I felt different this time round from when Bianca had presented me with a future of fatherhood. If I had taken the time to analyse things, I might have begun to see what had already happened. I might have seen that I had fallen hopelessly in love with you.'

All his cards were on the table and he felt good. Whatever the outcome. He carried on before she could interrupt with a pity statement about him not really being the one for her.

'And I may not cry at girlie movies or bake bread but you can take me on. I'm a good bet. I'm here for you; you know that. I'll always be here for you because I'm nothing without you. If you still don't want to marry me, or if you want to put me on probation, then I'm willing to go along because I feel I can prove to you that I can be the sort of man you want me to be.'

'Probation?' The concept was barely comprehensible.

'A period of time during which you can try me out for size.' He had never thought he would ever in a million years utter such words to any woman. But he just had and he didn't regret any of them.

'I know what the word means.' The thoughts were rushing round in her head, a mad jumble that filled every space. She wanted to fling her arms around him, kiss him on the mouth, pull him right into her, jump up and down, shout from the rooftops—all of those things at the same time.

Instead, she said in a barely audible voice, 'Why didn't you say sooner? I wish you had. I've been so miserable, because I love you so much and I thought that the last thing you needed was to be trapped into marriage to someone you never wanted to see out your days with.' She lay back and smiled with such pure joy that it took her breath away. Then she looked at him and carried on smiling, and smiling, and smiling. 'I knew I was falling for you but I knew you weren't into committed relationships.'

'I never was.'

'That should have stopped me but I just didn't see it coming. You really weren't the sort of guy I ever thought I could have fallen in love with, but who said love obeys rules? By the time I realised that I loved you, I was in so deep that the only way out for me was to run as fast as I could in the opposite direction. It was the hardest thing I ever did in my entire life but I thought that, if I stayed, my heart would be so broken that I would never recover.'

'My darling… My beautiful, unique, special darling.' He kissed her gently on the lips and had the wonderful feeling of being exactly where he was meant to be.

'Then I found out that I was pregnant, and after the

shock had worn off a bit, I felt sick at the thought of telling you—sick at the thought of knowing that you would be horrified, your worst nightmare turned into reality.'

'And here we are. So I'm asking you again, my dearest—will you marry me?'

They were married in Ireland a month before their baby was born, with all her family in attendance. Her father, her brothers and her brothers' partners all filled the small local church. And, when they retired to the hotel which they had booked into, the party was still carrying on, as he was told, in typical Irish style. And just as soon as the baby was born, he was informed, they would throw a proper bash—the alcohol wouldn't stop flowing for at least two days. Alessio had grinned and told them that he couldn't wait but that, before the baby discovered the wonders of an Irish bash, she or he would first have to discover the wonders of going on honeymoon, because they had both agreed that wherever they went their baby would come as well.

And their baby, Rose Alexandra, a little girl with his dark hair and big, dark eyes, was born without fuss, a healthy eight pounds four ounces. Rachel, who was over the moon at the prospect of having a sibling she could thoroughly spoil, could barely contain her excitement when she paid her first visit to the hospital and peered into the little tilted cot at the side of Lesley's bed.

The perfect family unit, was the thought that ran through Alessio's mind as he looked at the snapshot picture in front of him. His beautiful wife, radiant but tired after giving birth, smiling down at the baby in her arms while Rachel, the daughter he had once thought lost to him but now found, stood over them both, her dark hair falling in a curtain as she gently touched her sister's small, plump, pink cheek.

If he could have bottled this moment in time, he would have. Instead, still on cloud nine, he leaned into the little group and knew that this, finally, was what life should be all about.

* * * * *

Available October 21, 2014

#3281 REBEL'S BARGAIN

The Chatsfield

by Annie West

Injured in a skiing accident, there's only one person Orsino can turn to...his estranged wife, Poppy. They have unfinished business, and as the blazing passion between them reignites, Orsino's left wondering—will Poppy's sensual touch kill...or cure?

#3282 A VIRGIN FOR HIS PRIZE

Ruthless Russians

by Lucy Monroe

Romi Grayson once infiltrated Maxwell Black's cast-iron defenses then walked away. Now this Russian tycoon will stop at nothing, even blackmail, to have Romi warm and willing in his bed. And her innocence will make his long-awaited possession even sweeter....

#3283 PROTECTING THE DESERT PRINCESS

Alpha Heroes Meet Their Match

by Carol Marinelli

Princess Layla craves escape from her gilded cage—she wants to experience *everything* forbidden! The exception? She must remain pure for her future husband. Mikael Romanov swore to protect her, but as Layla gets beneath his skin can Mikael protect her from himself?

#3284 TO DEFY A SHEIKH

by Maisey Yates

It isn't the first time Sheikh Ferran has faced the edge of an assassin's blade, but soon his beautiful assailant is at his mercy. Now Princess Samarah Al-Azem must decide: imprisonment in a cell...or in diamond shackles as the sheikh's wife!

HPCNM1014RA

#3285 THE VALQUEZ SEDUCTION

The Playboys of Argentina

by Melanie Milburne

When Argentinian polo player Luiz Valquez rescues innocent Daisy Wyndham, the press reports they're engaged! It's a dangerous charade: with Luiz doing his best to be good and Daisy trying to be bad, how long before someone gives in?

#3286 ONE NIGHT WITH MORELLI

by Kim Lawrence

Eve Curtis is determined to remain independent and is happy keeping men at a safe distance. Until now. Because when Draco Morelli sweeps her off her feet, he opens her eyes to a whole new world of sin and seduction....

#3287 THE RUSSIAN'S ACQUISITION

by Dani Collins

Alesky Dmitriev's revenge plans backfire when he discovers that his new mistress, Clair Daniels, is a virgin! Undeterred, he's set on enjoying the perks of his purchase. Clair, however, is destined to be much more than just this Russian's acquisition.

#3288 THE TRUE KING OF DAHAAR

A Dynasty of Sand and Scandal

by Tara Pammi

Nikhat Zakhari's desertion once drove Prince Azeez to recklessness, but now he must choose: spend life in the shadows of the past, or embrace his future. He *must* assume the crown—but will Nikhat agree to be his desert queen?

SPECIAL EXCERPT FROM

Presents

Maisey Yates introduces you to a spectacular desert world, full of passion, excitement and secrets in the sand! Read on for an exclusive extract from TO DEFY A SHEIKH...

* * *

"I would much rather find a way for you to be useful to me." He slid his thumb along the flat of her blade. "But where I could keep an eye on you, as I would rather this not end up in my back."

"I make no promises, sheikh."

"Again, we must work on your self-preservation."

"Forgive me, I don't quite believe I have a chance at it."

Something in Ferran's face changed, his eyebrows drawing tightly together. "Samarah."

He'd recognized her. At last. She'd hoped he wouldn't. Not when she was supposed to be dead. Not when he hadn't seen her since she was a child of six.

She met his eyes. "Sheikha Samarah Al-Azem, of Jahar. A princess with no palace. And I am here for what is owed me."

"You think that is blood, little Samarah?"

"You will not call me little. I just kicked you in the head."

"Indeed you did, but to me, you are still little."

"Try such insolence when I have my blade back, and I will cut your throat, sheikh."

"Noted," he said, regarding her closely. "You have changed."

"I ought to have. I'm no longer six."

"I cannot give you blood," he said. "For I am rather attached to having it in my veins, as you can well imagine."

"Self-preservation is something of an instinct."

"For most," he said, drily.

"Different when you have nothing to lose."

"And is that the position you're in?"

"Why else would I invade the palace and attempt an assassination? Obviously I have no great attachments to this life."

His eyes flattened, his jaw tightening. "I cannot give you blood, Samarah. But you feel you were robbed of a legacy. Of a palace. And that, I can perhaps see you given."

"Can you?"

"Yes. I have indeed thought of a use for you. By this time next week, I shall present you to the world as my intended bride."

* * *

Don't miss
TO DEFY A SHEIKH,
available November 2014.

HPEXP1014-2